# Ghost on the Shore

LILY FOSTER



SHOREFRONT BOOKS

*Also by Lily Foster*

## THE LET ME SERIES

Let Me Be the One

Let Me Love You

Let Me Go

Let Me Heal Your Heart

Let Me Fall

When I Let You Go

## THE BLACKBIRD SERIES

When the Night is Over

Your Hand in Mine

Ghost on the Shore

All Your Life

This is a work of fiction. Names, characters, places and incidents are either the product of the author's imagination or used fictitiously. Any resemblance to actual persons, living or dead, events, or locales is entirely coincidental.

Copyright © 2021 by Lily Foster

All rights reserved. No part of this book may be reproduced in any form or by any electronic or mechanical means, including information storage and retrieval systems, without written permission from the author, except for the use of brief quotations in a book review.

First paperback edition January 2021

IBSN 9780998916774 (paperback)
ISBN: 9780998916767 (ebook)

Cover: Megan Barker Designs

# Ghost on the Shore

# Part One

ALL YOU LEFT BEHIND

# Chapter One

Grace Dawson is a liar.

And that is the gospel truth.

That I'm so good at it is no consolation. You'd think that as the days turned into weeks, then months and then years, it would get easier to stand in front of the mirror and look myself in the eye, but that's not the case.

I do it. I tell that woman with the sad eyes looking back at me that she did the right thing, the only thing she could have done at the time. *It was another lifetime*, I tell her. *Move on, for God's sake.*

Then I swipe on some lipstick and paste on a smile. Greet the day.

I pop into my aunt's house on my way to work. Make her some tea and sit with her for a few minutes until her home health aide comes in for her shift. Auntie Viv is not long for this world, but still I won't tell. And if I won't tell her, which would be as good as putting those words into a vault, then I suppose that I am planning on taking this secret to my grave.

Settling back behind the wheel again, the bright morning

sun catches on that diamond. It's heavy on my finger, and glitters in a way that's garish. I have to remind myself that a normal person would see that sparkle as a promise of good things to come.

I didn't want to say yes when Jack asked me. I wanted to tell him the truth, give him an out, let him know exactly who I am, but the words died on my lips. I couldn't believe my own ears when I heard myself say yes.

*Yes, I'll marry you, Jack.*

My teeth clench as I pull into my spot in the faculty parking lot thinking back on it. It was another Hallmark movie-worthy performance on my part. Have I become so good at faking it that people can't see even the slightest trace of sadness in my eyes? Given that despair is my default mode nowadays, it's hard to believe that I'm still capable of keeping up this charade.

To everyone in this town I am Grace Dawson, beloved high school teacher. I'm the plucky, optimistic educator amid a sea of ready to retire cranks. The one who spouts positivity until I'm blue in the face. The one who always gives her students a safe haven, a shoulder to cry on, or tough love when it's called for. To my adoring fans I march to the beat of my own drummer. I look on the bright side and I dream big.

Not everyone is a fan. No, the few remaining members of the old guard on the school board would like to see me gone. They're all fire and brimstone, spouting nonsense about how I promote reckless and promiscuous behavior among our town's youth. Do my students see me at Church on Sundays? Rarely. But I'm not working the pole at the local strip club either. The school district's teenage pregnancy and high school drop-out rates were far above the national average long before I came onto the scene, but some people are always looking for a scapegoat.

They don't approve of the books I pick to read in class, they don't approve of the uniforms I signed off on for the dance team, they don't approve of the way I dress, the way I teach—the complaints they've lodged are too many to list. Let's just say that they've tried to bully me into leaving for years but I'm not going anywhere.

It's not that I want to stay here. This isn't exactly some cosmopolitan mecca. It's a small town without the small-town charm and appeal you read about in those cozy romance books.

When you're born and bred somewhere you get used to it, you stop seeing your surroundings with fresh eyes. But I'm not from here so I see it all. I see the unkempt front yards, littered with boats that haven't been out on the river in years, and rusted-out cars that will never be fixed. I see the storefronts that were shuttered years ago on Main Street with the faded *For Lease* signs still taped in their dirty windows. I see the same look of desperation that I wear mirrored in the eyes of the working-class people of this town. From their appearance you can tell that some of them have given up entirely. Not Grace Dawson, though. I'm an outsider. I'm not like them.

Jack thinks this ring will lure me up to Pittsburgh, that I'll give up my job in this underperforming school for the greener pastures of a better district. That's what being married to him means, doesn't it? That I'll leave this place, free myself from the ties that bind me to this town.

Standing on the bank of the river, I pick up a rock and toss it in. She's not here and neither is he, so why do I stay? It's not like I can't be found. A few keystrokes on a computer, that's all it would take in this day and age. I don't need to stay close to the address I wrote on those forms so many years ago.

This isn't even the same river.

It looks just like it, though. When I lay back on the grass I can remember what it felt like to be there with him. When I wade in up to my ankles I can imagine those nights spent swimming, taking risks for the first time in my life. When I feel the freezing rain and the wind biting my skin in the dead of winter, I remember what it felt like to mourn, the devastating physical power of grief.

"Will you wait for me?" he used to ask.

"You know I will. How can you even ask me that question?"

With both of my hands in his that last time, he took a step back and raised his arms out to the side. "Look at you. You'll have guys beating a path to your door once I'm gone."

I pulled out of his grasp and wrapped my arms around my middle. "Don't say that. It's not true."

He came closer, turned me around so I was facing the water and wrapped me up in his arms. "You don't see what I see, Gracie. I don't know why that is, but I'm going to make it my life's mission to change what you see when you look in the mirror."

It's not like I thought I was an ogre or something. I knew I was pretty, knew men looked at me. But I was never comfortable in that skin.

I decided way back when that pretty girls come in two varieties. There were the girls who owned it, the ones who flaunted their beauty and might even use it as a weapon. They were the queen bees, the ones who slayed men and left them battered and bruised in their wake. And then there were girls like me. The ones who couldn't get a handle on it, who never learned how to harness the power their beauty could wield. It brought me unwanted attention when I was a kid, so

I grew up viewing it as a weapon that men could use against me.

"I don't want you to leave."

He rested his chin on my shoulder. "Believe me, no one's rethinking their life choices more than I am at the moment."

"How soon can you get back? I mean for a visit or leave, or whatever they call it."

"I wish I knew that, but you know I don't. I don't even know when I'll be able to call."

I nodded with tears in my eyes because I did know, he told me all of this before.

He kissed my head, and it's as if I can still feel it right now, can still feel the warmth of his breath and that feeling of security I had when I was in his arms.

"Remember what I told you to do?"

"Write to you."

"Every damn day, Gracie. I don't care if you write just to tell me what you had for lunch."

"Really? You'd be happy hearing about a ham sandwich?"

"Yep. Especially if you slipped in a picture of you with your mouth wrapped around it ready to take a bite." I elbowed him and he laughed. "Seriously, the days and weeks can drag when you're over there. No one understands how boring it can get. When you're in the middle of a shitty stretch, especially when you're in-country, mail call is the highlight of the week for most of us...or the month."

I turned to face him. "You get your mail once a month sometimes?"

"Only when we're off the grid. Most of the time it's not like that. But still write to me because a big stack of letters will get me through it when I'm missing you."

I did write to him, more times than I'd care to admit. They

started out upbeat. I told him every interesting thing my professors said, told him about the parties my roommates dragged me to, and I did tell him about the fabulous new gyro place that opened up off campus, so I did relay what I was eating for lunch. I got one letter back to every seven or eight I wrote. He warned me, but it's hard not to feel ridiculous when you get little to nothing in return.

I tore that first envelope open, excited and nervous at once. He was grateful for my letters, he told me. He thanked me for the pictures I sent, told me he missed my beautiful face so much that it physically hurt him.

The second letter came weeks later. He loved me, he wrote, and I cried when I read those words. Was I sure, he asked me, still sure that I'd wait for him? I shook my head, smiling. I didn't even need to think about it. Of course I would wait.

I got one more letter, and it was of the short and sweet variety. I still wasn't sure what it was that he saw in me, so his quick, impersonal note left me feeling unsettled.

I was still that girl, not even twenty years old, who didn't have the confidence to see myself objectively, let alone in a positive light.

I kept writing long after his letters stopped, but the tone of my letters changed too. They went from sounding like they were penned by an upbeat cheerleader, to concerned, and then when I heard nothing back, my letters turned matter of fact and then sterile.

*I need to speak with you, are you allowed to call me?*

*It's really important. Please call.*

My last letter was one single line: *I'm due in the middle of August.*

I never got a response.

"Do you think I'm making a mistake?" I ask him now as I

look down at the ring. "I'm thirty-three...Not getting any younger."

It comforts me to talk to him this way. I'm free on the bank of the river, speaking to a ghost, spilling my secrets. Because it's true what they say: dead men can't tell tales.

"I still haven't told Jack." I can practically see him shaking his head. "He won't understand. Now? No, I can't tell him now."

The wind picks up, rustling the leaves. I imagine the sound is his voice telling me: *There will never be a right time, Gracie.*

"She turned fourteen this past August. *Fourteen*. Can you believe it's been that long?"

The wind, the leaves—no one has an answer for that one.

And that's when I wrap my sweater tight around my shoulders, back away from the water and make my way to the car.

I don't trust myself sometimes.

I used to tell myself that I had to stay strong. For what reason, I still don't know. The weak voice inside of my head assures me that I have so much to live for: my students, my family, Jack and the future he has mapped out for us. But I'm so tired.

Lying wears you out. Living a false life, presenting some persona to the world that's practiced and phony? It feels like struggling against the current in chest-deep water every damn day.

It's a bone-weary kind of tired, and it's enough to pull you under if you let it.

# Chapter Two

*FIFTEEN YEARS AGO...*

## GRACE

*Mr. Brightside* is blaring over the speakers, so I have to ask him to repeat himself when he says, "You're popular."

"What?"

"I said," he leans in, "you're popular. I've been trying to talk to you for the past hour, but some guy always cuts in right before I can get to you."

He points to his ear and then gestures to move away from the speakers, and for some reason I follow. My roommates abandoned me a while ago, left me to fend off the last two guys who offered to buy me drinks in a way that left me feeling borderline harassed, so I don't feel the need to check in with them now.

We're down at the other end of the bar now, and while it's never quiet in this off-campus dive, we don't have to scream over the music to be heard back here.

"What's your name?"

"What's yours?" I shoot back, feeling uncharacteristically ballsy.

He smiles and shakes his head. "Damien."

"Like the kid in the movie?"

"Oh, I don't get that one too often," he deadpans. "Have you seen it?"

"Before my time."

"Then take my word for it, it's disturbing. I'm named after my uncle, otherwise I'd ask what my parents were thinking."

"It's actually a nice name. It suits you."

"I look devilish?"

I reach up to touch the dimple on his left cheek. "Maybe a little. But I mean it, Damien is a nice name."

"So?"

I don't even know this person, and I usually get all stiff and uncomfortable when unfamiliar guys approach me, but for some reason I can't help but smile when I answer, "Grace."

"That's a beautiful name." He looks genuine when he repeats my words back to me, "It suits you."

I look behind me to see what's causing all the commotion, and figure that the team everyone is rooting for must have scored or won or something. I have to get up on my tip toes so he can hear me when I say, "I've never seen you here before."

"I've never been here before so that makes sense."

"You're a comedian, huh?"

He shakes his head. "No, ma'am. Never been accused of being the slightest bit funny." He leans in to be heard above the noise when a group of guys start cheering again. "I'm just thanking my lucky stars that you're even talking to me right now. I watched you turn down one guy after another before. Thought maybe I was just lining up for a smack down."

I've been told that I come off like a cold fish on more than one occasion. *What, you're too good to talk to me?* Or the words that cut like barbed wire tonight: *Just asked if you wanted a drink, didn't ask for your hand in marriage, bitch.*

I look away from Damien. "I'm not like that."

"I'm just saying that I'm flattered."

He's teasing me and I don't like it. "I have a brother. I know it's not easy for a guy to walk up to a girl and ask if she wants a drink or if she wants to dance. I'm never rude when I say no."

"I never said you were rude." When I don't answer he leans in. "Hey, I didn't mean anything by it, I swear."

"Some guy called me a bitch tonight. He asked if I wanted a drink, and when I thanked him but told him no, that I was here with my friends, he didn't take no for an answer. I'm always nice about it but guys do that a lot. Am I supposed to say yes, encourage the guy waste ten bucks on a drink that I don't want? What if I'm not interested?"

"I guess I never looked at it from a woman's perspective. Walking up to a girl and getting shot down does suck, but you raise a good point." He looks to the empty beer bottle I put on the bar a moment before. "And just for the record, I never asked if you wanted a drink."

"That's right, you didn't. Guess I can't shoot you down then."

"Oh, you can," he says as he signals the bartender for another round, "because I'm dying to kiss you right now."

I cough and laugh at the same time. "Excuse me? You don't even know me."

"I like everything you've showed me so far." He hands me a bottle. "No pressure, though."

I take a long pull off my beer to quell my nerves because

I'm about to do something *way* out of character. "Come here, Damien."

He takes one step closer, then another. There's less than an inch of space between us when I angle up towards him and touch my lips to his. One strong arm slips around my waist and slowly draws me in closer. He makes a satisfied humming noise when I'm pressed up against him, and then he takes over, using his other hand to cradle my head and hold me close as he nips and licks his way into my mouth.

I choose to ignore the voice in my head screaming: *Get a hold of yourself, Grace!* because my Lord, Damien is a good kisser. Not too soft, not too forceful, not too sloppy, but just the perfect amount of wet. I'm up on my toes again and his hands have slid down to cup my ass. And then he makes contact, presses the front seam of his jeans up against mine. I can feel my eyes flutter, open then close again, the sensation so good that I feel damn near faint.

From behind Damien I can hear a few people clapping, then a girl's voice calling out, "Can you say slut?"

He breaks the kiss and turns on them. "What did you—"

"Damien?" She looks surprised before covering her mouth to hide her smile. "I didn't realize it was you." Still amused, she looks me over. "Maybe you two should get a room or something?"

One of the morons who started that lame slow clap is now practically doubled over laughing. The other guy slaps Damien's back. I'm sure my cheeks are burning a crimson shade of red while all this good-natured bro ribbing is going on, and as the seconds tick by, I am so regretting my decision to lock lips with this stranger.

Damien clears his throat. "Guys, this is Grace. Grace, these are my buddies, Andrew and Eli." Looking to the girl who threw down the slut comment and still hasn't apologized, he says, "This is Eli's sister," before turning his back on her.

The sister, who looks like a dead ringer for Penelope Cruz—so picture brown hair and brown eyes like me, yet *nothing* like me—puts a hand on his shoulder and wedges her way back into the group. "Rude, Damien. Aren't you going to properly introduce me to your new friend?"

"Grace, this is Gianna."

"Hi, Grace. Nice to meet you."

I don't need intuition or a sixth sense to tell me that Gianna is not a genuine sort of person. She still has her hand on Damien's shoulder, she's sticking her chest out, has her head cocked to the side like she's challenging me, and her smile is doing a poor job of masking the snarky, condescending vibe she's giving off. She's a character right out of that movie, *Mean Girls*, so ridiculous that it's comical.

"Is it?"

"What?"

Now she's looking at me as if I'm slightly deranged. And maybe I am. On any other given day, a girl like Gianna would intimidate me. I steer clear of people like her. But tonight I'm different. I'm the kind of girl who can talk and flirt with a guy without second guessing every single thing I say. I'm the kind of girl who will make out with a handsome stranger in the back of a bar. Tonight I don't take any crap.

"Is it nice to meet me?"

Damien clears his throat and steps closer to me. "I'm thinking Grace might be offended by that comment you made. I know I was." The hand he had resting on my hip now begins to caress that spot, and I decide that I like him even more now than I did a minute ago.

She looks to him. "Are you being serious right now?"

His eyes soften and something passes between them that makes me feel excluded. "It just wasn't called for, G."

He has a nickname for her. He knows her well.

Gianna hesitates as if she's wrestling with something before turning to me. Her smile is bitter and forced when she says, "Sorry if I offended you."

She looks to him again for some unspoken cue and then rejoins her brother and the other guy, now closer to the bar.

"I think I've made an enemy for life."

"Her bark is worse than her bite," he says, taking a slight step back.

And with that step, the air shifts. She broke the spell we were under, ruptured the nice, safe bubble he had me in.

I look down to where his hand still rests on my hip. He removes it, runs that same hand through his hair. And in that instant I revert back to the person I am, knowing the only reason I looked down to my hip was to compare my chunkier build to that other girl's body. And when I compare myself to her I no longer feel good enough.

I look around the bar, trying to spot one of my roommates. "I think I'm going to go."

"Grace?"

I don't want to look at him, don't want him to see the shame and disappointment in my eyes, but he places a finger on my chin and coaxes me. "I'd like to see you again if that's all right."

"Um," I resume my search of the bar, "maybe I'll see you around?"

"That's doubtful. I don't go to school here."

That gets my attention because although I don't know his friend Gianna personally, I have seen her on campus. She's one of those girls who have the best looking guys on campus following her around like fools. Gianna falls into that first category: she's a beautiful girl and she owns it.

"I just figured since, um, Gianna goes here."

He smiles. "So you *do* know her?"

"Not really. I've just seen her around."

He takes a sip of his beer. "I was in basic training with her brother, Eli. He's like family to me."

"You're in the military?"

"Marines." He gestures to Eli. "I re-upped, he didn't. He just started school this fall. Oldest freshman on record."

"You guys don't look so old."

"I'm joking. He's only twenty-two. I'm twenty-four. I did two years of college before I enlisted. I'll be twenty-seven when I get out."

"Sounds like prison."

"Some people see it like that, I guess. Not me, though."

"Obviously, since you reenlisted."

He nods, takes another sip of his beer. "So can I do more than just see you around?"

"We're outta here!" my roommate Frannie calls out from behind me. "Hurry up...Car's outside waiting."

"I don't know. I mean, you're leaving, right?"

"I am, but not for six weeks."

"Grace!"

I turn around and hold up one finger as I shoot Frannie a look. "It was really nice meeting you, Damien." Looking to where Gianna is standing with her brother and a crowd of other guys, I smile. "I mean, it was *truly* nice to meet you, but—"

"But you're letting me down easy. And you *are* being nice about it."

I feel awful and torn and tragic, already missing this person

I hardly know. I shake my head, looking down at my shoes. "I have to go."

He calls after me when I'm just a few steps away, "What's your major, Grace?"

"Biology, why?"

He shrugs. "I'll see you around."

# Chapter Three

## DAMIEN

She's going to think I'm a psycho.

This is day three of my mission. I'm sitting on a bench that's situated between Redman Hall and Wilson Hall, reading a book that I'm not actually reading, trying to look like I'm minding my own business as I conduct surveillance.

I usually have way more intel at my fingertips when I'm trying to track someone down. All I've got right now is a first name and the location of the biology department. I could press Gianna to find out her last name, but even though the clock is tick, tick, ticking, I'm not that desperate—yet.

She looked like the cat that got the cream Sunday night when she spotted Grace walking out of the bar and away from me. When Eli asked, "Where's your girl going?" she could barely contain her smile.

Eli and I have weathered the kind of shitstorms together that either bind you to someone for life, or make it so that you never want to lay eyes on them again. Eli and I are brothers. His family has welcomed me in, let me stay at their home more times than I can count on both hands. So it should be, and I *so* wish that Gianna looked at me like a brother, but that's not the case. And I've got no one to blame for that but myself.

For the next six weeks I'm crashing at Eli's apartment, so I'll be seeing her more regularly, I suppose. I plan on doing everything I can to make things cordial while not putting myself in the position of having any sort of alone time with her. I don't want to confront her about her behavior, don't want to fight with her—I just don't want. It's bad enough that Eli thinks she has a massive crush on me. I mean, it wouldn't end our friendship or anything, but he'd be ticked off if he knew I'd kissed her once upon a time when I was drunk.

She was eighteen. I don't blame her. I was twenty-two and should have known better. I felt bad for her when she got dumped by her boyfriend the day after prom. I never got the details—as I said, I was pretty drunk—so I just assumed she'd been wronged. That maybe the kid was some asshole who broke it off because G didn't put out. I still don't know what happened, but now that I've gotten to know Gianna better, I'm thinking it's more likely that she drove that poor kid to kick her to the curb.

She's not nice to people she doesn't know. It's almost like she has to size someone up and see what they bring to the table before she decides whether or not she likes them.

Lucky me, I've been deemed worthy, but I've seen her dismiss people based on their looks, their social standing or their parents' line of work. I saw her look at a guy's shoes once and smirk. She's a snob with no reason to be one. Gianna is what my mother—God rest her soul—would have called a *five and dime millionaire*. I can picture my mother rolling her eyes, chiming in with another one of her favorites: *That one, she's a real Bronx debutante.*

Gianna sized Grace up on Sunday night. I watched her. Watched as she got that superior look on her face. Probably told herself she was better than Grace, when in my eyes nothing could be further from the truth.

I was like a heat-seeking missile when I spotted Grace from across the bar. Long brown hair, curvy little figure, kind eyes. Yeah, I saw her turn down a guy or two, and saw the way it pained her to do it. It's like she was unaccustomed to attention, which doesn't make any sense, or maybe she was used to it but it still made her uncomfortable.

I did feel like I was setting myself up to be turned down, but the life I've led so far has me giving absolutely zero fucks. Life is short, so you best get busy living or get busy dying. And Grace set something off inside of me, like a promise of something good to come. Three days later and I'm still thanking God she didn't send me off with my tail between my legs. And even though she did ultimately turn me down and walk away, I could see the indecision in her eyes, the disappointment when I told her I'd be gone in six weeks.

*Take a chance*, I wanted to tell her. *So much can happen in six weeks.* And now I'm down to five weeks and four days, growing impatient as I turn into another piece of furniture dotting the campus green.

Gotta come up with a new plan. Improvise, adapt and overcome.

"Damien?"

"Hey, Grace." I close the book, stand up and try to play off the whole *funny running into you here* thing, but I'm not really concerned about blowing my cover. Like I said, no time to waste.

"Are you waiting for Eli? Is he a science major, too?"

"Close, he's an engineering major, but I was actually hoping to run into you."

"Oh." She looks away but can't hide her smile. She's pleased, which pleases me to no end.

"Are you on your way to class or do you have time to grab lunch?"

"I have an hour before my next class."

"Can I take you to lunch?"

She looks up at the clock tower. "It's ten-thirty."

"Early lunch, late breakfast, whatever."

She tugs her bag higher up onto her shoulder. "Sure." She gestures to the left and starts walking. "I know a place."

"Let me carry that, it looks heavy."

"Thanks."

"Jesus, do you lug this around from class to class all day?"

She giggles, and I must be stupid or something because I'm finding her ridiculously adorable right now. "Wednesdays are my long days." We turn and she leads me down a set of stairs into a basement cafeteria. "They have decent sandwiches here. I usually get the roasted veggie panini."

"That sounds good. Are you a vegetarian?"

"No, I eat everything."

And once the words are out of her mouth, I notice her pulling the hem of her shirt down over her butt as her face colors.

*No, don't do that*, I want to tell her. *You're perfect, don't you see?*

"Like a million years ago I dated a girl who used to ask the guy at our local bagel store to scoop her bagel out before toasting it, and she'd only eat egg whites and ask him not to use butter or oil. I mean, whatever floats your boat, but the poor guy was a fry cook and the place was always jammed. It got to the point where I'd see him cringe every time we walked in the door."

That gets her to laugh. "I should probably go that route, but I don't think I could eat an egg sandwich if it didn't have bacon and cheese on it."

"That's what I like to hear."

She leads us to a table. "You want to check out the menu?" she asks, gesturing to the list of items written on a blackboard.

"Nah, what you're having sounds good. I like to eat as many greens as possible when I'm on leave. You do get some really good meals, but as a rule, the food sucks once you're deployed."

"Canned beef, stuff like that?"

"The MREs aren't like they used to be." I answer her confused look. "Meals ready to eat."

"Oh."

"But they're nothing to write home about." When I ask her what she wants to drink, she offers to pay with her student meal plan. "Not happening."

"Aye, aye captain."

I set her bag down on a chair and stop cold when I see ballerina shoes jammed in along with her laptop and a full change of clothes. "You're a dancer?"

She blushes. "Getting back into it, I guess you could say."

"Nice. I'll be right back."

Grace takes the bottle of water I hand her and then pauses in the middle of unwrapping her sandwich. "I'm still kind of shocked that I ran into you."

"Thought you'd never see me again?"

"Kind of."

"Are you happy you did?"

She nods once. "I didn't like the way things ended the other night."

"Neither did I. That's why I've been roaming around campus like a creeper for the past three days."

She covers her mouth, laughing around the mouthful of food she's chewing. Eyes wide, she asks a moment later, "You've been looking for me?"

"I told you I'd see you around and I meant it."

"You got lucky."

"I did."

"No," she shakes her head. "I mean, you got lucky because I'm hardly ever on this side of campus."

"Eli told me this is where most of the science and engineering classes are."

She looks down into her lap. "I have a confession to make." When she meets my eyes again, she looks worried for some reason. "I'm not a biology major. I'm supposed to be, and my parents believe that I still am, so it's just what usually pops out of my mouth when people ask. I changed my major after my first semester last year."

"You never told them?"

She lets out a cheerless laugh. "No. My parents are both doctors, so it's just expected that I'll follow along the same path."

"What are you majoring in?"

"Education. I want to be a teacher."

"That's great. You don't think they'd be cool with that?"

"They would *not* be cool with it. In fact, they'd cut me off if they found out."

"How have you managed to keep it from them for so long?"

"They're super busy, the both of them. The downside is

that my parents have no time for their children. The upside is that I pretty much do what I want."

"They don't look at your grades?"

She shakes her head. "I'm what they consider to be average. Don't get me wrong, academics have always come easy to me, but there's smart and then there's gifted. When I didn't get into their alma mater, they kind of stepped away and focused their energy elsewhere." Blessed with parents who always had my back, I can't easily wrap my head around this and I guess it shows in my expression. "They're not terrible people," she assures me. "And when they do find out they'll get over it. My brother is the golden child. He's brilliant. They'll still get their doctor."

"How old is your brother?"

Her smile tells me she loves him and that they're most likely close, and just that has me falling for her a little bit more. "Aiden is sixteen. He won some major national science competition last year, which is like, an amazing thing to do as a high school sophomore."

"That's impressive."

She nods as she chews. "It's beyond impressive. He's already been approached by department heads from some of the top schools in the country, so he takes most of the pressure off me."

"So maybe they'd be fine with the teaching thing."

She shakes her head. "They're big on the whole *those who can't do, teach* philosophy. Well, unless you're teaching future doctors or research scientists." Her eyes twinkle when she adds, "But they actually look down on those professors, too. My mother did a stint at Johns Hopkins when she was on maternity leave and *still* talks about the experience as if she was some oracle gracing them with her vast wealth of hands-on experience. My mother and father are intellectual snobs."

"I don't think they'd approve of a college dropout like me."

Grace studies me for a moment. "No, they probably wouldn't, but don't take it personally. And if it's any consolation, I like you."

"I'm good with that."

"My plan is to break it to them over Christmas this year. You know, when everyone's feeling all joy to the world-ish."

"Sounds like a good plan. Except you'll be home for a few weeks, right? That could be rough. Maybe you should wait until they pay next semester's tuition and then tell them as you're walking out the door on the last day of break."

Grace cocks her head to the side. "You *are* a little bit evil, aren't you, Damien?"

"Just looking out for you, Gracie."

"Gracie." She looks lost in a memory for a moment before she comes back to me. "I had a teacher who called me Gracie. Miss Poole, my seventh-grade teacher. I loved her. It's weird... No one has ever called me that since."

"I've never had a nickname either. Kind of hard to shorten Damien."

"What's your last name?"

"Erikson.'."

"Damien Erikson...Has a nice ring to it."

"So does Grace Dawson."

"Did I tell you my last name the other night?"

"Nope." I don't tell her that I can see her name written on the top of an envelope stuffed into her bag. "That required a little digging on my part."

"I don't know if that should make me feel special or stalked."

"Pursued sounds so much better."

She laughs. "Pursued. Yeah, it makes stalking sound romantic."

"After you left the other night, I was asking about you. Gianna probably knows your blood type and your social security number, but she was no help."

Grace's smile fades. "Oh."

And I should have known better than to mention the very same girl who ruined the other night.

Looking to change the subject, I ask, "So where does dancing fit into all this? I don't know much about dance, but I'm assuming you have to be pretty hard core to get up on those pointe shoes."

"You know they're called pointe shoes, so you know more than you're letting on." Smiling, she looks me over, leaning back so she can take in my lower body. "But me thinks you're too brawny to be a danseur."

"Busted." Easy to talk to, sharp, and she's got a cute sense of humor. Check off another few boxes in Grace's favor. "My mother worked at Lincoln Center—"

Her eyes light up. "Lincoln Center? That's amazing!"

"Whoa there, Nellie. She *cleaned* Lincoln Center, she wasn't on the board of directors or anything."

"Still...It's such a magical place. I've been there a few times and I just love everything about it."

"I got to see a few performances. I'd act like my mother was dragging me there when she was able to wrangle a few matinee tickets for the shows that weren't sold out, but I enjoyed it."

"What did you see?"

"I got to see *Serenade*—"

"Oh, I *love* Ballanchine!"

"And I saw *Pharoah's Daughter*. I remember really liking that one."

She nods. "It's trippy."

"Yeah. And *Swan Lake* was really good, too. My mother rarely got tickets to the big ones like that."

"It's everyone's favorite for a reason."

"What's your favorite?"

She smiles like she's remembering something good. "La Bayadère."

"See, I don't know so much. I've never heard of that one."

She nods. "That would be a hard ticket to get. Always a sold-out performance at Lincoln Center, I'd imagine, no matter who was dancing the lead."

"What's it about?"

"Love." Grace smiles in a way that makes me want to lean across the table, take her face in both of my hands and kiss her. "There's Nikiya, the temple dancer. She's in love with Solor, a noble warrior, and he loves her. She's also loved by the powerful High Brahmin but doesn't love him in return." She clutches her hands in front of her heart. "It's got it all...Love triangle, betrayal, desperation. Lots of drama."

"Have you ever danced the lead?"

"Once." She looks away and her smile drops when she catches sight of the clock. "My class is on the other side of campus. I've got to get a move on."

"I'll walk you to class." I gather our stuff and take it to the trash. "Ready?" I ask as I heft her bag over my shoulder.

"Sure you don't mind carrying that?"

"Not at all."

And the conversation is easy for the next few minutes as we make our way across campus. There are no awkward silences, no having to come up with things to say. When her steps slow

I know we've arrived at our destination, and I'm more than just a little disappointed. Already strategizing, I barely register what she says when she asks, "So, this six weeks is like a vacation?"

"An extended leave that I requested between tours."

"A break is good, right?"

I don't tell her the reason behind it because that's a story for another day. I just say, "It's turning out to be a good thing," because that is the God's honest truth. I feel like something good is coming, something life changing, and I can't attribute this weird sense of divine promise to anything or anyone but Grace.

"Here we are." She looks as disappointed as I feel when she says it.

"There's a good band playing tomorrow night at a small place in Durham. Can I take you out?" She hesitates for just a second, but it's one second too long. "You're not going to make me hack into the school's operating system to get a copy of your schedule so I can accidentally on purpose run into you on campus again, are you?"

She studies me. "For some reason I get the feeling you actually could do that."

"Sorry to disappoint. I've got some uncommon skills, but computer hacking isn't one of them."

"It's just that you're leaving pretty soon. I mean, is there any point?"

"A lot can happen in six weeks."

"Five weeks and a few days," she corrects. And now I know she's been thinking about me, so I go all in.

"I like you, Grace. A lot. And you're right, I'll be leaving in a few weeks, but I don't want to pass up on something that could be great just because the timing is sucky."

"Sucky." She gifts me with a soft smile and a nod. "I'll go out with you tomorrow."

I take my phone out. "What's your number?" I tap it in and then hear her phone buzzing a moment later. "Text me your address and I'll pick you up at seven. We'll get something to eat first?"

"Sounds good."

I look down to read her text. "You live on Darling Drive?"

"It's so random. The other streets are named Elk, State, Maple...Typical street names."

I'm tempted to comment on it as we linger outside for a few more seconds, but I know whatever I come up with will sound corny. I smile, though, because someone like Grace should live on Darling Drive. It fits.

"Maybe wear your hair up tomorrow night, ok?"

"Why?"

"You'll see."

# Chapter Four

GRACE

I have an elastic band in my bag, but my hair is not up. My wavy hair has done more than just cooperate today. I used some new anti-frizz product that coaxed bona fide curls from my unruly mane, so I'm not about to go and ruin the effect.

My hair is glossy perfection, my makeup is understated, and I borrowed a casual strapless dress from Frannie that makes me look fan-freaking-tastic.

"Jeez...I look kinda plain Jane in that dress, but you look—"

"Is it all right?" Turning back and forth in front of the mirror, I'm suddenly wondering if I've put in too much effort. "Too short you think?"

"You look amazing. Seriously, this guy, whoever he is, is going to drop dead when he sees you." We both start laughing. "Yeah, that wouldn't be good," she says. "I mean that he's going to lose his mind...In a good way."

Slipping my feet into a pair of strappy sandals, I look down and admire my shiny red toenails. I even splurged for a pedicure after class today. "His name is Damien."

She sits on my bed just as Reese comes in and joins her. "You look sexy, mama."

Frannie lets out a dreamy sigh. "Damien is a hot guy's name. I only got a quick look at him, but the name certainly fits."

"I kind of hate you a little bit right now," Reese says with a totally fake pout. "I tried to chat that guy up on Sunday night but he paid me no attention."

"This whole thing is crazy." I'm saying this to Frannie and Reese but I'm really talking to myself. "He's leaving in less than six weeks. I'm wasting my time."

"When is shagging a hot man ever a waste of time?" Reese points at me. "And notice I said man, not boy or guy or dude." Flopping back on my bed and fanning herself, she adds, "Damien is a *man*."

I think back to our lunch yesterday, to the way he held the door open for me and guided me inside with his hand on the small of my back, the way he pulled my chair out for me, and the way he carried my heavy bag. I noticed the muscled arms and torso underneath his fitted shirt, felt his rough stubble on my cheek when he kissed me goodbye, and took note of how small I felt in his arms when he gave me a quick hug. So he is a man, yes, but he's also a gentleman.

I drag in a deep breath when the doorbell rings.

"Want me to get it?" Frannie asks as she's jumping off the bed and making her way to the door.

I start to say that I'll answer the door but the two of them have already beaten me to it.

"Hi, you must be Damien," Frannie greets him.

"I am." He steps inside and nods his head as the girls introduce themselves. "It's nice to meet you both." Fixing his eyes back on Reese he says, "You look familiar."

She shrugs and smiles. "Oh, I'm the girl who tried to climb you like a tree the other night at the bar." Damien's eyes go wide and he coughs as Reese gestures to me and adds, "But you kept staring over at that one, so I gave up."

The things I love about Reese, that she's forward, outspoken and plays no games? Right now I'm wishing she'd take it down a notch. I'm nervous enough as it is.

"Sorry about that." Damien manages to say this to Reese with a smile that's both a comfort and a tease before turning his attention to me. "You look beautiful, Grace."

I want to say it back to him because he looks so good, but there is no word in the English language that fits. Handsome is too formal, good is too generic, and to tell him he looks downright edible—while true—would be all sorts of weird. I just go with a barely audible *thank you* instead.

"Where are you two heading?"

Frannie asks as if she's just making casual conversation, but she's the most sensible member of our trio. Damien doesn't go to school here and I know next to nothing about him, so Frannie is being Frannie: careful and wise.

"Rudy's for something to eat." He looks to me and asks, "Do you like that place? Is that all right?" When I nod he looks back to the girls and says, "Then we're seeing a band at Blue Note."

"Sounds good." Reese waves and winks as we're heading out the door. "You two kids have fun tonight."

"Yeah, have fun," Frannie calls after us, "pickles."

"Pickles?" Damien looks amused. "Is that your nickname?"

"No, that's our safe word." He looks to me with a raised eyebrow, and I full-on belly laugh when I realize I've just gone all Christian Grey on him. "Frannie likes to have a code word that we can text to one another if we're like, in trouble or something."

He nods. "That's smart."

Damien stops beside a motorcycle parked at the curb and then looks to me. "I'll drive slow. I was going to suggest that you'd be more comfortable in jeans and regular shoes, but you look so good, Grace. I didn't want you to change."

It takes me a moment to digest the compliment "I've never ridden on a bike before."

"I keep it at Eli's parents' house. You're not allowed to have any sort of vehicle on base during your first tour of duty and it's just not practical to have one now." He hands me the spare helmet. "Sure you don't mind?"

"No. It's warm out tonight and I like trying new things."

"That's my girl," he says as he fastens the strap under my chin for me.

I have to look away as he does it because those words do something to me. *My girl*. Having been in his company for all of what, maybe two hours total? I feel silly for wanting to be his girl. But I get no reprieve from this sensory overload. He helps me onto the bike, the skirt of my dress riding up to accommodate the seat, and then Damien straddles the bike, reaching back and grabbing my butt to scooch me forward so that I'm flush against him. I'm convinced he can feel my heart hammering in my chest when he takes both of my hands and wraps them around his waist.

"I'll drive slow," he assures me again as we pull out onto the road.

I can't hear anything except the sound of the engine as we drive, but my Lord, I can feel. There's basically nothing between my ass and the leather seat, and truly nothing between my thighs and the denim of his jeans. My hair is blowing in the wind, my hands are practically touching his torso through the fabric of his shirt, and the vibration of the engine is seriously messing with my ability to control myself. I press into him a bit when we take a turn and then move my hands across his middle as if I'm trying to hold on tighter. By the time we get to our destination, I'm flush faced and slightly out of breath.

"So how was it?"

"Hmm?"

"Your first ride on a motorcycle. How was it?"

Smoothing my dress down as he helps me off the bike, I manage to collect myself. "Yeah, I liked it."

He removes my helmet and then rubs my shoulders to warm them even though there is no need. "I'm glad you said yes," he says after a moment, and then takes my hand and leads me inside.

I know the hostess from my Modern American Lit class, so she gives us a prime table on the outdoor deck even though there are people waiting. She waggles her eyebrows as she hands us our menus, and Damien, who's none the wiser, looks at me like I'm a little looney when I giggle.

He runs a hand over his hair and asks, "What is it? Do I have helmet head or something?" And this makes me laugh harder because he's got hardly any hair to begin with.

"How could you get helmet hair with that crewcut?"

He rubs his hand over the top of his head again. "Yeah, that's one thing about the service that I won't miss someday. Not like I'd ever grow my hair long, but I'm a little tired of the high and tight look."

"No, you wear it well. I just can't imagine you with messy hair, that's all. Wait," I run a few fingers through my own hair, "do *I* have helmet head?"

He reaches across and takes my wrist gently. "Your hair looks great...Perfect."

A waiter comes by and takes our drink order. Damien asks for a water along with his beer and I hold my breath after ordering myself a vodka cranberry. I let out a sigh of relief when our server walks off without asking for ID.

"So Gracie, I know you're an education major, I know you're a ballerina—"

"A dancer, not a ballerina."

He nods. "A dancer. I know you like grilled veggies and that your nickname is pickles." That earns him a laugh. "But I don't know the basics, like where you're from or how old you are. Although I'm guessing you're not quite twenty-one from the way you ordered that drink."

"Busted. I'll be twenty in February. Most of the off-campus places turn a blind eye to the drinking age but Rusty's is tougher. I've only been here a few times."

"You're nineteen."

"For a few more months. When is your birthday?"

"August fifth."

"A summer baby."

He nods, still studying me as the waiter places our drinks on the table. There's not much on the menu at this place so I order ribs and Damien orders the fried chicken, which they claim is world famous. He orders mashed potatoes and kale salad for side dishes, and before thinking it through, I ask for a side of mac and cheese.

I take a sip of my drink and then shake my head. "You're going to have to roll me out of here later."

"After you roll *me* out of here. Pretty ballsy tagging your fried chicken as world famous. I couldn't pass that up."

"Oh, I'm from Philadelphia by the way. You asked where I was from before."

"Right. And I told you I'm from New York."

"What do your parents think about you being in the Marines?"

"Unfortunately, they're both deceased."

"Oh, I'm so sorry."

"Thanks." Damien reaches across the table to take my hand while I'm busy beating myself up for asking such an idiotic question. "And hey, it's all right. I've had a few years to work through it."

"I shouldn't have asked something so personal."

"It wasn't too personal. My mother died of cancer when I was in high school and my father died when I was halfway through my sophomore year of college. He was pretty much a mess after losing my mother, so I stayed close to home, commuted to Fordham instead of living in the dorms. The doctors said he died of complications related to high blood pressure, but I swear my old man died of a broken heart."

"They had a good marriage?"

"Solid." He nods. "They were best friends."

"That's kind of amazing."

"What are your parents like? I mean, I know they must be intelligent and driven if they're both doctors."

"Intelligent and driven, that's a good way to describe them. They're impressive, I'll give them that."

"But they're tough on you."

"They were tough on each other, really. And distant. But maybe that's not entirely fair. They both have demanding careers. Maybe it's hard to nurture a marriage when you're being pulled in so many different directions." I answer his unspoken question. "They got divorced when I was fourteen."

"Ouch."

I nod as I take another sip. "But like you said, I've had a few years to work through it."

"How do they get along now?"

"Pretty well actually, as far as the co-parenting thing goes. Hence the whole *they* will cut me off once they find out I'm squandering their money on a bogus degree."

I sit back for a moment as the server sets our plates down. It smells incredible, and I'm grateful when I see him drop a few hand wipes along with the extra napkins. Picking up a sticky rib, I tell Damien, "I'm probably going to have to bathe in those wet wipes after eating this."

"Bold choice for a first date. I like it."

"Yeah, maybe I should have gone with something a little easier to handle."

He closes his eyes and hums after taking a forkful of the mac and cheese. "So glad you ordered this. Nothing goes better with fried chicken than mac and cheese."

"Mac and cheese is pretty much the greatest side dish of all time. I don't care what the entrée is." I gesture to his plate. "So, does it live up to its world famous claim?"

He reaches over and puts the piece he just bit into up to my lips. And then holy mother, yes, he's feeding me. "I'm not exactly a connoisseur," he says as I chew the mouthful, "but I'd say it's up there with the best I've ever had."

It's crispy, it's smoky, and has the perfect hint of spice. My eyes fall closed as I swallow, and maybe I even moan a little. "That's soooo good. It's like fried chicken nirvana."

He nods, his eyes fixed on my mouth as he lets out a breath. "If it gets *that* kind of reaction out of you, then we're coming here for dinner tomorrow night, the night after that and then the night after that..."

I'm teasing when I ask, "You're looking into the future?"

He shrugs. "I'm just *not* looking to fix an end date on something that's just starting."

"Fair enough."

We eat in peaceful silence for a few minutes before he asks, "Do you really think your parents won't approve of you becoming a teacher?"

I nod. "One hundred percent. And if I tell them now they'll just try and force my hand... Maybe steer me towards research or biomedical engineering or something like that. I told you I was going to come clean over Christmas break but I'll probably chicken out."

"So what do you want to teach?"

"I love to read and I do some creative writing, so I'd like to teach high school English. My grand plan is to teach and also coach the dance team."

"We didn't have a dance team at my high school. I know I would have noticed if we did."

"Yeah, I'm sure you would have remembered," I tease. "And I can start a team or a club at whatever school I wind up at."

"You sound like you've got it all figured out."

"Hardly. I mean, I've never even said any of that out loud before." The waiter drops the check and walks away before I add, "You're easy to talk to."

"Thanks. A lot of people tell me that."

"Like who?"

"Uh, I was kind of the go-to guy for our unit. Trouble with your girl back home? The stress or monotony of the long tours getting to you? Go talk to Erikson." He smiles. "Maybe it's because I've experienced death or loss or whatever, but the guys would often come to me when they had a problem."

"That's a good quality, to be someone people can lean on."

He goes to take his wallet out of his back pocket and I gesture for him not to. "You got lunch the other day, I'll get this."

"Grace," he shakes his head in a way that tells me he's not having it, "I don't like that trend. If I ask you out for dinner, I'm paying. If you ask *me* out, same thing, I'm paying. I don't want to offend you or anything, but I mean it when I say it's my pleasure to take you out. Understand?"

"Fine, you win."

"Thank you."

He stands and reaches down to take my hand. "You ready?"

*Chapter Five*

DAMIEN

It's not like I have many to compare it to, but this might be the best first date ever.

Watching Grace eat barbecued ribs was a sight to behold, and the conversation during dinner flowed so easily, same as the last two times we were together.

And now, while the band was rocking before, they've slowed down some. They're playing a cover of Dawes' *Time Spent in Los Angeles*, and it's fitting that I'm standing behind Grace as she sways to the music while she is, indeed, wrapped up in my arms. I hesitated before going for it and touching her this way, but the bar is packed and she was standing so close to me that I figured she'd be down with it. Thank goodness she is.

It's been a long time since I've been with a woman, longer still since I've enjoyed the company of the woman I'm with the way I'm digging Grace. I keep reminding myself that I have to go slow, but damn, I don't want to. I want to soak up everything I can before going back to that lonely life, want to soak up every bit of goodness and light from this beautiful girl that I can.

She turns her head to look up at me. "This band is really good."

"Yeah, Eli told me about them."

"Eli's family is from North Carolina?"

I nod. "Right here in Durham."

"They could just live at home then. Couldn't ask for an easier commute."

"I'm sure their mom would love that, but Eli needs to be out on his own. He's too old to be home. And living in the dorms was the only way they got Gianna to stay in state. I think she wanted to go to Arizona or someplace like that."

"I could totally picture her at those Vegas-style sorority pool parties."

"She's not so bad, but yeah, I know what you mean." And I have no intention of ruining this night with talk of Gianna, so I'm definitely looking to change the subject when I ask her if she has class in the morning.

"I only have one class on Fridays and it meets at ten."

"What class?"

"Choreography."

"So you're studying dance, too?"

"Only a minor concentration. I take one dance class a semester, two at the most."

"I was right...You do have it all figured out."

"It doesn't feel that way."

I turn her around slowly and rest my hands back on the sweet curve of her hips. "I'd like to see you dance sometime."

She laces her fingers around my neck and tilts her head to the side. "We're dancing now."

She's looking up at me, and I can't take my eyes off of her

as we move to the slow beat of the music. Is this how it feels? What my father used to say about meeting the person you're meant to be with? It's like being thunderstruck while swimming in this peaceful feeling of faith and security.

I could stand here holding her forever, but at the same time I know it's not nearly enough. I need more.

The band stops after the song is over, thanking the crowd before the DJ starts back up. "Want to get out of here?"

"Yeah," she says on a whisper.

We're both quiet as we head back out into the night. For me it's a mix of nerves and anticipation. For Grace I'm thinking it's the same.

I take the leather jacket that's always rolled up and stashed in the compartment beneath my seat and gesture for Grace to let me put it on her.

"It's still pretty warm."

It is a mild night, but she's wearing next to nothing. I've never had a wreck, and at the snail's pace I've been driving tonight I'm definitely not worried, but I want to protect her in any way I can.

"Let me."

I slip her arms into my jacket and smile when I see the way the sleeves hang down over her hands. As I put her helmet on and fasten the chinstrap, I can feel her breaths coming in quick, chest rising and falling with each inhale and exhale.

Taking one step back, I school myself, tell myself for what's got to be the tenth time to slow down. *You'll scare her off.* But she turns the tables on me, wrapping her arms around my waist and pulling herself flush up against me once were settled onto the bike. Not two minutes into the ride, Grace decides to let her hands wander, skimming underneath the fabric of my t-shirt, and the feel of her hands on my skin is so unbelievably good.

She lets out a hoot and then laughs when I pick up speed on the open road. I'm still not going half as fast as I normally would, but it's enough to have Grace's hair whipping in the wind and enough to have me back to feeling free and hopeful.

I should just walk her to the front door, kiss her and then end the night on a positive note. Prove to her that I'm respectful and lay the groundwork for our next date. But she's looking at me, eyes searching. Grace doesn't want the night to end, same as me.

She turns away once we're on the porch, but there's no hesitation before she unlocks the door and leads me inside. The kitchen light is on but it's nearly midnight. There's no sign of her roommates.

"Do most sophomores live off campus?"

"I'd say most students move off campus *after* sophomore year." I take a seat on the couch as she turns a lamp on in the living room. She heads for the kitchen asking me, "Do you want a beer?"

"Sure."

"You hardly drank tonight."

"Two beers is my limit when I'm on the bike."

"Safety first," she smiles as she hands me the bottle. "I like it."

I tip my bottle to hers. "Thank you for tonight. I like hanging out with you."

"Same here." She takes a small sip and then sets her beer down on the coffee table. "So where are you staying while you're on leave?"

"I'm crashing on Eli's couch for a few weeks. His apartment is about a mile from here."

She looks me over. "You're kind of big to be crashing on a couch."

"A couch is downright luxurious compared to some of the sleeping arrangements I've had to endure over the past couple of years." I laugh, shaking my head. If this girl only knew some of the places I've sought shelter. I've slept outdoors wet and shivering my ass off, as well as covered in sweat and swatting flies off me while half conscious. "A couch is like a king-sized bed at the Ritz Carlton."

She's smiling. "I guess that was kind of stupid on my part."

I rest my free hand on her knee. "You haven't said one stupid thing since I met you."

"It's been less than a week," she teases. "Give me some time."

Looking around the living room, I tell her, "This is a nice place. The kitchen and living room are much bigger than Eli's." I turn back to her. "Why did you move off campus a year early? Did you hate the dorms?"

"I didn't hate it, it's just that freshman year you're assigned to a double, but I guess they had a bigger incoming freshman class than they'd anticipated so they crammed a third bed into most of the rooms. Three people in one tiny room is a lot. I mean, I think I made two friends for life with Reese and Frannie, but trying to get a decent sleep when one person has a habit of rolling in after midnight every single night can be a bit much."

"I'm guessing that was Reese."

"Good guess. She's night owl, even when she's just studying."

"So she's at the library now?"

Grace shakes her head as she sips her beer. "On a Thursday night? No, Reese is out painting the town red."

"Frannie too?"

"She likes her fun, but she's studying nursing. That's a tough major, so Frannie keeps her partying to the weekends."

"I don't know her at all, but she comes off as..."

"Sensible?" I nod and then she does too. "I'm sure she's been in bed since ten. We all have our own rooms here and it's sooo much better. I think one of us might have killed Reese if we had to repeat last year."

"I've never had my own room." Laughing, I add, "It's a life goal."

"So you have brothers and sisters?"

"No, just a really small apartment in the Bronx. A one bedroom with me on a pull-out couch in the living room."

She's wide-eyed, but that's my truth and I won't ever present myself as something I'm not to impress others. When Grace said she was from Philadelphia, I knew she wasn't referring to West Philly. From her clothes to her speech to her manners, it's clear that she's a Main Line girl. We grew up on opposite sides of the tracks.

"I've never been to the Bronx. What's it like?"

"We lived in a pretty nice neighborhood...Riverdale. My section was all apartment buildings, but ride your bike for a mile or two and it's like another world. Tree-lined streets, shiny new cars in every driveway and fancy houses. There are some beautiful Queen Annes."

"Queen Annes?"

"Big old houses with wrap-around porches and those round gables that make them look like something out of a fairytale. I'd ride around that part of Riverdale on my bicycle, picking out which one I'd buy for my parents someday."

"That's sweet."

"Selfish, really. I'd tell myself it was for them but I really just wanted a big grassy yard for myself."

She looks lost in thought for a moment before asking, "Fordham is pricey, isn't it?"

I nod. "Scholarship. I had a full ride."

"And you gave that up?"

"My father worked at the World Trade Center. He worked nights as a custodian, so he was already gone by the time the planes hit that day, but he lost a few close friends."

"That's awful."

"Fordham lost a lot of alumni, too. And I guess I was just restless, sitting in a classroom while so much was going on. Then when my father passed away I just felt…I don't know, destined for something. So I settled his estate." I pause, laughing. "I'm using the word estate in a purely legal manner. There were no properties to sell or heirlooms to put into storage." She reaches over and takes my hand, rubbing her thumb over it in a way that comforts me and encourages me to go on. "I took a leave of absence from school, enlisted, cleared the apartment out, and the next thing I knew I was at Parris Island for basic training." I look at her and smile. "The rest is history."

"You've led a pretty amazing life for someone who's only twenty-four."

"I'm no different from anyone else. Everyone has a story."

Grace takes both of our empty bottles and brings them to the kitchen. I'm about to tell her that I don't want another one when she comes back into the living room empty handed. She stands in front of me for a moment and then slowly lowers herself down, her knees straddling my hips. "Is this all right?" she asks.

There's no need to answer. Grace knows from the feel of me underneath her when I pull her in closer, and in the way I take her face in my hands and gently tilt her head to kiss her. I want her. She knows this.

She kisses me back, and I swear it's never felt so good—never before in my life. Her lips are soft and coaxing me. My hands are rested on her thighs where her dress has ridden up, and the combination of her skin and her kisses is working me up. *Slow down*, I remind myself, and then gently break the kiss and pull back.

Her hands are on my shoulders and her smile is soft.

"You're so beautiful, Grace."

She shrugs. "I'm average."

"No." I push a lock of her long hair behind her ear. "How could you ever think you're just average? Your eyes, your smile..." My eyes drift south without my permission. "Everything about you is so *not* average."

She pulls at the stretchy smocked top that's keeping everything in place. "Being above average in that department pretty much tanked my dance career back in high school."

"What do you mean?"

"Long and lean, that's the ideal. There's been all this empowerment talk in the past couple of years, and there are some successful dancers who have more muscular builds, but most of it is talk and nothing more. My teacher, Miss Abramov, started giving me the stink eye once I hit puberty."

"Seriously?"

She's laughing when she says, "Tits are not desirable."

"Speak for yourself."

That earns me a belly laugh, and the sight of her laughing is something I find myself wanting to photograph just so I can keep it with me and look at it forever.

"Miss Abramov was a beast."

"Sounds like it."

"Too fat, too short, too curvy…She body shamed pretty much everyone who didn't have her perfect ballerina build. She even told one girl that her head was too big. I mean, you can starve yourself to lose weight, but you can't do anything about the size of your head. Stella…I still remember that girl running out of the studio crying."

"That's harsh."

She nods. "It's one of those things I can look back on now, and maybe not laugh about it, but recognize the absurdity of it all. But back when I was a kid? She said some things that definitely messed with my head."

"I don't like Miss…"

"Abramov."

"She sounds like a nightmare."

"She's pretty typical in the world of classical dance. I'd say more than half of the girls in our school had an undiagnosed eating disorder."

"That's awful. I mean, I'm actually getting pretty fucking angry right now."

"Simmer down, big guy. As you can see, I don't starve myself anymore."

I run both hands over her hips and give a gentle squeeze. "Promise me you never will."

She raises her palm in a pledge. "Scout's honor. I could never last more than a week back then anyway. I'd be ripping into a bag of sour cream and onion chips after a few days on hard-boiled eggs and iceberg lettuce."

"Makes me see that world through a different lens."

"It's all about sacrifice and aiming for perfection, but yeah, that world can be pretty cruel." She gives me a gentle poke in the chest. "What about you? I saw that movie, *Jarhead*, and I could barely get through it."

"Agreed." I laugh thinking back on it, but harsh doesn't even scratch the surface when it comes to recruit training. "I guess there are similarities...Basic training can be a psychologically damaging experience for some people."

"I wouldn't last a day," she says absently, her hands moving from my shoulders to rest on my pecs. "I know I still view myself with an overly critical eye, but I'm over it for the most part."

"The thought of someone criticizing your shape, or anything about you, is just insane. I mean it, Grace, you're gorgeous."

She blushes and turns her head. "Just kiss me again, will you? Compliments make me twitchy."

"Yes, ma'am."

And it's hard to put the brakes on again once this kiss gets started. She's pressed up close, every tender and needy spot on my body lining up with hers, and then she's moving her hips in a way that has me going mad with wanting her.

She breaks the kiss. "Let's go to my room."

"Are you sure?"

Grace nods her head and breathes out when she says yes. She's had two drinks—no, three when I count that beer. She doesn't seem buzzed but I'm still not sure about this.

Once we're in her room and she starts shimmying out of her dress, I have a moment of clarity. I don't want to rush this thing between us.

"Grace."

She looks back up as she's easing one foot out of her sandal. "This is awkward, but do you have anything? It's been a while. And when I say a while, I mean it's been a *long* while. I haven't had sex since I was fifteen."

*What?*

I don't even know what to do with that comment, and my silence makes it worse. She looks up at me shame-faced. "I...I don't have a lot of experience."

I pat the spot on the bed next to me. "Come here." When she sits, I take her hand. "I really like you. And I'm not looking to push you or rush into something you're not ready for." I hand her the silk robe that's draped over her desk chair and she puts it on. "Believe me when I say that I want you, but I don't want to hurt you."

She nods, biting her lip with her head cast down.

"Who was it?" She looks to me, confused. "When you were fifteen...Who was it?"

"Just some boy." She takes a deep breath. "My dance instructor's son."

"Miss—"

"Abramov...Yeah. He wasn't around all the time but he'd help his mother out at the studio sometimes."

"How old was he?"

"Peter was a junior in high school, so I guess he was seventeen?"

"And you were a freshman?"

She nods. "Talk about easy pickings. My father had just moved out a few months before, and on those rare occasions when my mother *was* home, she was swilling red wine. On top of that, Miss Abramov was making my life a living hell." She lets out a cheerless laugh. "All he had to do was tell me I was pretty."

"Is that why compliments make you twitchy?"

"I don't know." She turns my way and then backs up, tucking one leg up underneath her to get more comfortable sitting on the bed. "He happened to be at the studio on one of the more particularly brutal days. His mother was ripping into everyone. And when she got to me she looked at my chest, disgusted," Grace shakes her head at the memory, "and then told me I was no longer dancing the lead that I'd been promised. She told me I was better suited for *that jazz studio over by the mall*. That's like the ultimate insult to a classically trained dancer...Same as telling me to go work the pole in a strip club."

"What a bitch."

"Well, no one would describe her as warm and fuzzy." She scoots back again, creating some distance as she settles in and rests against the headboard. "Peter caught me as I was walking to the bus stop. He called his mother the c-word, which made me laugh, and told me not to listen to a word she said. He told me I was the best dancer in the troupe, the only one he couldn't take his eyes off of." She smiles but it's one that's laced with hurt. "He was smooth."

I move opposite her, resting against one of the posts on the footboard and then nod, gesturing for her to tell me more.

She shrugs in response. "You know how this ends. I started skipping dance practice, Peter would meet me at his house after school when his mother was busy at the studio, and I gave it up because he made me feel good."

"He took advantage of you." She thinks on that for a moment and then nods. "Did he force you?"

Grace shakes her head. "Took advantage, used me? Yes, I'd agree with that. But he never forced me." She swallows before admitting, "I liked it. I mean, I felt cursed by this woman's body I was getting but wanted *no* part of, and then Peter comes along and he's totally mesmerized by my hips, my breasts. All the things I was ashamed of, he made me feel desired because of them."

"You said fifteen, so I'm assuming this didn't go on for too long."

"A couple of months, almost four," she says as she counts it off on her fingers. "Prom was a huge big deal at my high school. Like, ridiculous when I think about it. That promposal trend may have even started at my high school."

"Prom what?"

She laughs. "You know, where the guy does some ridiculous stunt and publicly asks the girl to prom?"

"Never heard of it. I went to a small Catholic high school. We had a prom but I didn't go."

She looks devastated on my behalf, which makes me laugh. "You didn't go?"

"Nope. Only the boys with steady girlfriends went. It was kind of lame. I don't think I missed out on anything."

"My senior prom date asked me by having a pizza delivered to my house with the word prom and a question mark written in pepperoni."

"That's actually pretty funny...and creative."

"He was a friend of mine and I kind of knew it was coming, so yeah, it was really great. We had guys running across the soccer fields during games with signs asking girls to prom, and one kid got suspended for sneaking into the school secretary's office and asking over the loudspeaker."

"Ouch."

"Double ouch because the girl didn't want to go with him."

"That's a lot of pressure, on the guys *and* the girls."

"It's gotten crazier with every passing year. Last spring I heard that a boy from my school paid every kid on the marching band to show up at some girl's house at the crack of dawn on a Sunday morning while he stood on her porch dressed in a tux with a bouquet of roses.”

“I’m sorry, but that just sounds stupid.”

“I’m giving you some background just so you understand how big a deal it was.” Grace puts the back of her hand up to her forehead and acts like she’s fainting when she adds, “So you’ll understand just how traumatized I was when Peter told me he’d asked someone else to his junior prom.” She lets her arm drop and cracks a smile. “He was smuggling me over to his house like three times a week and I’d totally romanticized the entire thing, so I was beyond annihilated. Oh, and she just happened to be gorgeous and sweet and the most popular girl in the junior class.”

“What a jerk.”

She looks away and her eyes fix on her phone. “It’s after one o’clock in the morning. Seriously, I usually don’t drone on like this and monopolize conversations.” She laughs and looks at me shaking her head. “I’m sorry. You must be thinking I’m in need of a skilled therapist.”

“Nope. I’m just thinking about how I’d love to slap the shit out of Peter.”

“He apologized to me.”

“He did?”

She bites her lip and nods. “I ran into him this summer. I was walking out of a store and he was coming down the street. Totally random. Anyway, he asked me to get coffee with him and then basically told me that he still feels bad about what he did to me. He was sincere. I could tell it really had been weighing on him.”

“So you forgave him?”

“I did. There’s no use holding on to that kind of stuff.”

“You’re nicer than I am.”

"I don't get that vibe from you. I think if you were in my shoes you would have forgiven him, too." After a moment she says, "So now that I've ruined the evening..."

"You didn't ruin anything. I'm kind of honored you shared all of that with me." I stand up. "But I should probably head out. It's late and you've got class in the morning."

"Yeah," she says absently.

"Can I see you this weekend?"

She's teasing when she asks, "After hearing all that? You still want to see me?"

"Were you trying to scare me off or something? If you were it didn't work." She doesn't answer right away, and I force a smile to mask my disappointment. "If you want to hang out this weekend, call me. I know you're busy with studying and everything, so no pressure."

"It's Frannie's birthday tomorrow night, so we have a girl's night planned, but maybe we can meet up for the football game on Saturday?"

"You have tickets to the game?"

"No." She laughs like I've just said something absurd. "I went to the season opener last year and haven't been inside the stadium since. I was talking about the tailgate parties."

"Eli mentioned it. I think his sister's sorority is having something but I want no part of that."

"You'd skip a party at Delta?" I can tell she's teasing even before she adds, "*The* most exclusive sorority on campus?"

"Happily."

"Ok, then it's a date."

"I'll be late, though. I'm working with Eli's dad until around three."

"Where?"

"Mr. Oliveri is a general contractor. I'm just doing some basic carpentry at one of his project sites."

"How did you learn to do that?"

"Trial and error." She winces when I hold up my left hand and show her the spot where I nearly shot clear through my hand with a nail gun. "My father did side work on the weekends. He taught me a lot."

"That looks like it hurt."

"I think I was too freaked out to feel actual pain at the time. But I enjoy that sort of hands-on work. And helping out makes me feel like I'm repaying Eli's parents for all the times I've crashed at their house."

She gets up and comes to where I'm standing. The robe she's wearing just skims the tops of her thighs and the silky fabric is molding to every curve she possesses. I know it's better to say goodnight now, but I'd be lying if I said I didn't want to push that flimsy robe down and off her shoulders.

"I had a good time tonight, Grace."

"Me too."

She lifts up on her tip toes and I dip my head down. "You're making it hard to say goodbye," I tell her after kissing her. And she is. She's got her arms laced around my neck again, so I know without even looking that her barely-there robe has ridden up to her ass and I can feel her chest pressed up against mine.

She takes a step back, cheeks flushed and breathing deep. "I'll see you Saturday."

*Chapter Six*

GRACE

"Are you up for an adventure this weekend?"

I'm on my bed, smiling as I think back to the steamy adventure we had last weekend. "I'm up for anything."

"You sure about that?"

"Hmm...Are you talking skydiving or something?"

"Nothing like that. Just camping, but I know some girls aren't into sleeping outdoors."

"I've never been camping before but I'm up for it."

"That's my girl. It's going to be warm and I know of a nice spot that's off the beaten path. There's decent hiking and it's right on the river."

"What should I bring?"

"A bathing suit, sweats for late-night, a towel, some sunblock...I can't think of anything else right now."

"Is this like a campground that has bathrooms and showers?"

"That's not camping," he says. "I want you to have the real

experience. We'll catch our dinner, cook it over an open fire and we'll get clean in the river."

"Oh...kay."

"It's one night, Gracie girl."

Gracie girl or just plain Gracie. I smile every time he calls me by that nickname. It makes me feel special, makes me feel like I'm his.

It's been two weeks since our first official date. Two weeks since I sat on my bed half-dressed and spilled all of my secrets to Damien. He knows me better than the family and friends who've known me all my life.

In the light of the morning after, I convinced myself that I'd scared him off. Poor Grace, a damaged little girl who's been looking for love in all the wrong places. She lies to her parents because she's desperate for their approval and she lets boys use her because she sees herself as unworthy. That's not who I am. Maybe that's who I was at fifteen, but I'm not that girl anymore.

But I let him in, showed him everything ugly and embarrassing—everything I regret.

When he texted that he was waiting for me outside the fine arts building the next day and asked if he could take me to lunch, my heart just about melted.

Damien is kind. That first night in the bar when he shut Gianna down and defended me I knew it, and he's shown me kindness every day since.

"I guess I can rough it for one night."

"No, Gracie girl, you're tougher than you think. I think you could survive in the great outdoors with me for weeks."

"We could be like those contestants on *Naked Survivor*."

"Huh?"

"You've never seen that show?"

"Never even heard of it."

"Damien, it's crazy! I'm not even sure if that's the name of the show, but it's like *Survivor* except way more intense. It's a guy and a girl who meet for the very first time when they're dropped off in some jungle, mountain range or a desert, and then they get naked and have to survive for, I don't know, a month with nothing. No food, no bottled water, no shelter. It can be brutally hot or freezing cold. They have to make fire, find water and figure out a way to make it drinkable, and they have to catch and kill their food."

"They do all of this naked?"

"Yes, it's bananas!"

"Hmm...Maybe we'll give it a go this weekend. I'd like to get you naked and see if we can survive the elements."

"In your dreams." I cringe thinking back to one particularly brutal episode. "They get covered in bug bites and scratched by branches in places that look, um, uncomfortable."

"Wait. How do they keep warm at night?"

"Body heat, baby."

"Seriously?"

"It never seems like the people hook up, though. Which is weird because they're as naked as the day they were born."

"Now I'm thinking we definitely have to try this out."

"You want me buck naked with you in the tent, huh? We *are* sleeping in a tent, right?"

"Yes, we have a tent...But there's no pressure, Gracie."

I never should have mentioned Peter and the whole having sex at fifteen thing. I massage my forehead with my free hand, trying to erase the memory. Ugh, I told Damien that I liked it, too. That I wanted it when I was too young and too easily manipulated to make good decisions for myself.

"Right." Desperate to change the subject, I ask, "How is Eli doing?"

Damien told me that part of the reason he got permission for this unconventional leave was because of Eli. He was vague on the details but shared that Eli was struggling towards the end of their last tour. He wanted to help him transition back into civilian life. I don't really get it, he has his family and hometown friends here for support, but I'm grateful for whatever circumstances brought Damien into my life.

"He's doing well. I think going back to school has been good for him. The classes keep his thoughts focused on something productive. He's in a good place."

"That's good to hear."

I decide not to press for more, to hold back from asking what it is that I really want to know. *What happened during that last tour?* I know that life isn't easy. It's dangerous, I know at least that much. It's been less than three weeks but I already care about Damien. I want him to reassure me that he'll be safe, to make promises that are impossible to keep.

I'm a realist. Like I said, I'm not that same overly trusting, naïve fifteen-year-old girl who used to believe in insta-love. But I'd be lying if I said I wasn't falling for Damien. I live for those hours after class when he takes me for rides on his bike, when we grab something to eat or just sit on the couch together watching television. I love it when he shows up to walk me home from class, love it when he pulls me onto his lap when we're with Eli and his friends. And when I cooked dinner for him last weekend and he swore it was the best chicken marsala he's ever had, it made me so ridiculously happy. I want to please him, want him to think I'm beautiful, special and too hard to resist.

Too difficult to leave.

But I know he's leaving. That's not up for debate. So I tell myself to live in the moment. To wring every bit of goodness and joy that I can out of these next three weeks.

"All right, I'm all yours this weekend, Sergeant Erikson."

"All mine," he says. "I like the sound of that."

# Chapter Seven

DAMIEN

"You up for a run?"

Eli is still in bed and it's after ten o'clock. I've already been for a five-mile run, showered and grabbed coffee with Grace before class. He doesn't have class until noon today, but this laying around all day shit has to stop.

"Eli." I give him a not so gentle nudge. "Get up."

"My alarm is set for eleven. Leave me alone."

"No can do. Get up. We're taking a run."

He murmurs something that sounds like *fuck off,* but then gets out of bed scowling on his way to the bathroom. He doesn't look especially happy as he's tying his running sneakers, and curses once we hit the street and he realizes he forgot his sunglasses. I'd say he's acting like a child, but that's an insult to children the world over.

I break the silence once we're about a half-mile into it and have a rhythm going.

"I'm heading to Lejeune on Monday."

"What for?"

Eli, who was in tip top shape just a month ago, is having trouble keeping up with me. He's drinking too much, sleeping in, and generally adopting a piss poor attitude.

"Meeting with Staff Sergeant Barre."

"Why? You still have three weeks left."

It will only be two weeks and four days as of Monday, but I'm trying not to focus on that.

"I get the feeling that I won't be stateside for too long once I'm back in."

"I'm surprised they gave you time off just to babysit my sorry ass."

"Shut up."

He slows our pace to a jog and I let him. "You know exactly what I'm talking about. Let's not start lying to each other now, all right?"

"You'd do the same for me."

"But you'd never need that from me. That's the difference between us."

"We had a bad stretch. Everyone in the unit was struggling towards the end."

"I still can't stop thinking about him."

I'd ask if he means Cooper, but I know damn well that's who he's been fixated on. "You did everything you could...We all did."

"He took the easy way out. That's what I keep telling myself, Damien. It's the only thing that keeps me from..."

"You went to your appointment yesterday, didn't you?"

"Yes, Dad."

"Don't joke about that, asshole."

He nods and then slows to a stop. "The therapist tells me to picture my mother, my father and Gianna whenever it gets really bad. Not like to lay a guilt trip on me or anything, but just to remind me that it's the people you leave behind who suffer. It's easy to leave. Maybe not easy, but there's an end."

I put a hand on his shoulder. "Coop's parents...I can't imagine that kind of pain. Promise me, brother."

He doesn't promise but at least he nods, and I have to be satisfied with that.

I'd like to tell him what his life looks like to an outsider like me, but that's not what he needs. Eli knows he has a great family, knows he has friends who care about him, knows he has a good future if he wants it. But that's the one thing no one can fix for him. *He* has to want it.

It's not like I came out of that tour unscathed—not one of us did—but some of us fared better than others.

"I feel like a broken record, Eli, but I need to keep saying it. Adequate sleep, good diet, exercise, sticking to a daily routine, laying off the booze, listening to your doctor—"

"You're not wrong. It's just that having to be so mindful, as my doctor would say...I don't know. It makes me feel like, yeah, I *am* a mental case. Like I'm not capable of living a normal life. I mean, why the fuck am I so sad? I didn't come home in a box or a fucking wheelchair."

"You're sad because that was a sad place. You're home but that doesn't mean you leave all that shit behind when you board the plane."

As we climb the steps up to his apartment, he stops and turns to look at me. "Why are you going back there?"

"If you asked me last month I would have told you why, but I'm not so sure anymore."

And I'm grateful he doesn't say anything. No opinions, no advice. I want to avoid all talk on the topic.

"Finally! I was starting to think I cooked all this food for nothing."

Gianna is standing in our kitchen wearing an apron like she's the picture of domestic bliss, spooning scrambled eggs onto three plates. There are fresh blueberries on the side and some slices of avocado. She can be a pain in my ass, but she makes an effort where her brother is concerned. I'm grateful for that.

"This smells great." I look to her and grant her a smile for the first time this week.

"Thanks, G. I'll be right back," Eli says as he heads to the bathroom.

"Just like you said...Healthy fats, high protein and happy foods."

"The blueberries, yeah. I read somewhere that they combat depression.

"How is he? He looks a little bit down."

"He's not over the hump yet."

"You didn't get humped yet?" Eli slaps me on the back. "All those dinners out and you still haven't sealed the deal? Time waits for no man, Erikson. You best get to tapping that."

Gianna sets the bottle of ketchup down on the table with unnecessary force. "Gross, Eli." She says this to her brother but she's scowling at me.

"I'm just kidding. Grace seems really nice."

I don't look up at either of them as I pepper my eggs. "She is."

She's more than nice. Grace is also a good sport. That first weekend after our date, I planned to meet Grace and her friends at a house party after the football game. I mentioned it in passing to Eli, knowing two of his hometown friends were planning on hitting the party at Gianna's sorority house with him. I don't know why I was surprised when Gianna texted me with some fake emergency less than an hour after I met up with Grace. That's how she operates. Gianna knows Eli is my Achilles heel. Hint at the slightest bit of trouble where he's concerned and I'll drop everything. She knows this.

She wasn't tipsy when I got there, not even close. The laugh, the falling into me crap? Phony as hell. Her eyes were clear, her reasoning skills fully in tact. I'm trained in intelligence gathering, trained to read body language, trained to detect even the slightest change in a person's expression or breathing pattern. But I didn't need any of that to read her. I could smell the lie from a mile away. And Eli was fine. He was nursing his beer, talking to some girl—best I've seen him in weeks. No, Gianna was being a brat, plain and simple. She wanted to ruin my night with Grace and she succeeded.

Gianna reaches across and takes the pepper shaker from my hand before I can put it down. "Too bad you're leaving in three weeks." She tilts her head to the side when I look up. "Seriously," she says, her words laced with false sincerity, "I feel bad for both of you. I wish you had more time." When I don't answer, she goes on to plant the seed. "There are parties most nights of the week around here. You can't expect that Grace won't move on. I mean, she's no different than anyone else, but I do hear that Grace and her friends are, um, *regulars* at the frat houses."

"You heard that, did you?"

She shrugs her shoulders. "College life. That's how it is for some girls."

Eli looks to ease the tension at the table. "You got your eye on anyone special, G?"

"Nope." She looks down to her plate like she's sad, and I

have to hold back from starting a slow clap and announcing: *And the Oscar goes to...Gianna Oliveri.* She shakes off her pain —gag—and grants her brother a soft smile. "Most of the guys I hang out with are really immature. Anyway, I'm focusing on my work this year. I have to keep my grades up or I'll get booted out of the nursing program."

"I'd say most of the guys at that party last week were all right. One or two jerks, but most of them were fine."

Eli looks off into space, something he's taken to doing the past couple of months. Everyone needs to reflect and think, that's fine, but he can sometimes do it mid-sentence.

He comes back to us not half a minute later, takes another drink of water and looks at Gianna. "But you should focus on your work. Nursing is no different from pre-med. Those classes are no joke."

Eli looks between me and his sister. I still think he'd be pissed if he found out about my momentary lapse in judgment a couple of years ago, but I'm fairly certain there's a part of Eli that would like nothing better than for me to become a part of their family someday—an *official* member of the family. Ugh.

"How are your classes going so far?" she asks Eli. And when I look down at my plate and see the sliced avocado and the blueberries, see the care she took to bring her brother a fresh, healthy breakfast, my anger cools.

"So far, so good. As long as the professors don't go running at the mouth, spouting off on shit they know nothing about, then I'm happy."

"I don't follow," Gianna says.

"Nothing. Gets me aggravated just thinking about it." He takes a calming breath. Looking to me, he changes the subject. "What are we doing this weekend?"

My priority is supposed to be Eli, I know that. And while I

don't resent him for needing my support, I feel like I'm constantly torn between this sense of duty I have to help Eli and my desire to spend every last moment I have here with Grace. I've only known her for a few weeks, so it's crazy to feel the way I do about her, but it's how it is. There are never enough hours in the day to satisfy my need to be with her, and I pretty much always feel like I'm being pulled in opposite directions. I'm trying my best to do right by Eli but there are times, like right now, when it's hard.

"I've got plans on Saturday but let's do something Friday night." I ask Gianna, "Know of any good bands playing tomorrow?"

"Not off the top of my head, but I'd be down for that. But I'd also be down for a quiet night, just catching dinner and a movie."

"I wouldn't mind laying low tomorrow night either. I want to check out the rugby game on Saturday. Some guy in my European History class asked me if I might be interested in joining, so I figured I'd go watch and see what it's all about."

I tell him, "That's great," without thinking it through, and get an eye roll in return. Yeah, I was a tad too enthusiastic there.

"So," Gianna gets up and goes to rinse her plate in the sink, "movie night here and take-out, or do we hit the town?"

"Just come over here," Eli tells her. "I'll order from that sushi place you like. And you can ask your friend Kayla to come if you want."

"Oh, I can ask *Kayla*?" she teases.

He stands and scrapes his plate into the trash. "Yes, wiseass. You can ask your hot friend." Turning to me, he clears his throat and adds, "Ask Grace if you want."

"Or don't," she says under her breath. Piping back up, Gianna smiles like it's no big deal, but it's clear that she's annoyed. "If you two are looking to double date, just say so. I'll stay home."

"Gianna's right. Let's just have a three amigos night."

It's so damn hard to smile while clenching my teeth. "Sounds like a plan."

# Chapter Eight

## GRACE

I could get used to this view.

It's hot today. Like, August kind of hot. It's usually mild in North Carolina this time of year, no need for more than a light sweater at night, but today it's humid and it's got to be in the mid-eighties.

Did he strip his shirt off on purpose? Does he want me to suffer, sitting here with nothing to do but watch as his muscles flex and strain with the effort it's taking to chop wood for the fire pit he just made by digging a hole? No portable grill, so I guess we'll be cooking pioneer style. Damien means business.

"I can help, you know."

He glances back and smiles. "Almost done."

"I thought you were a commander of men. Command me, Sergeant. I want to help."

He trades the axe for a mallet, using it to reinforce the four corners of the tent, then tosses the tool into the back of the truck before coming to stand before me. Reaching a hand down to pull me up he says, "Time to catch us some dinner, Private Dawson."

I do my best to imitate the crisp salute I've only seen in movies. "Aye, aye, Sarge."

"It's aye, aye, Sir," he corrects, swatting my ass. "And let's ease up on the lingo. I don't want any reminders of my other life this weekend. I feel like I'm on borrowed time as it is."

That shuts me up quick. Borrowed time is right. We only have two weeks left as of this Wednesday.

I guess I'm still sporting a sour face when I look up. He keeps hold of the fishing pole he was about to hand off and comes in closer. "Don't think about that. We have this beautiful day together," he says as he raises his chin, gesturing for me to look out over the river, sun-kissed and glistening. "Let's focus on right now."

"Don't borrow sorrow from tomorrow," I whisper.

"That's a good one. Words of wisdom from your mother?"

I shake my head and smile. "My mother is a lot of things. She's smart, fierce, independent...But a philosopher? No." Taking the pole from his hands, I head towards the water and he follows. "Those words of wisdom are from my Aunt Vivian, my father's older sister."

"Did you spend a lot of time around her growing up?"

"Off and on, and then I spent an entire summer with her a couple of years ago. The summer after I gave up dance. My brother was heading to some camp for child prodigies and I didn't want to do anything but sit home in front of the television and lick my wounds."

"I'm thinking that wouldn't be acceptable in your house."

"You'd be right. But I refused to step foot in the dance studio, and I told my parents I'd run away if they forced me to go on the summer abroad program they were pushing." He baits my hook and hands the pole back to me. "They didn't know what to do with the drama queen I was morphing into back then."

"Pretty standard behavior for a teenager, isn't it?"

"I don't know."

Damien holds me back when I go to cast my line. "Here, do it this way," he says as he steps behind me and then guides me hand over hand. Moving in close, he lowers his voice. "I have big plans for tonight...Don't want to spend it in the emergency room with a hook in my face."

He pecks my cheek when I laugh. "You know I have absolutely no shot at catching us anything suitable to eat, don't you?"

"I have faith in you, Gracie. And I only found one fishing pole in the Oliveri's garage, so our fate is in your hands."

"No pressure."

"None whatsoever."

"What's in this river, anyway?"

"It rained yesterday so we have a shot at some bass, largemouth and Roanokes. But we're more likely to catch pickerel or crappies."

"What did you have for dinner, Grace? A *delicious* filet of crap."

"That's c-r-a-p-p-i-e, sweetness. And filet of crappie when it's seasoned just right? It *is* delicious. You'll see."

"I might just stick to the side dishes."

"What side dishes? I told you, we eat what we catch, hunt or pick."

"Pick? Is there a secret garden up here or something? Is that where you're going to source the fresh herbs required to season your world-famous crappie?"

"Uh, I may have cheated just a little."

"Really?"

"You *need* salt. That's just...You can't cook fish without it. And I brought along some pepper, some cilantro, a few limes—"

"Limes? Wow, we're really roughing it."

He's laughing when he points his finger at me. "I was thinking of you! Figured I'd make you a nice cocktail, let you sit back and relax after a tough day of fishing and hiking."

"And the cilantro, Bobby Flay? Were you thinking of me when you stashed that in your secret little cooler?"

"You'll thank me later."

"You'd never last a week on that show." I turn my head to look back when he doesn't respond, and I'm rewarded with the sight of Damien's shorts dropping to the ground. My breath hitches and my body heats in an instant. He is perfection. "I was only teasing, you know. That wasn't a challenge."

He looks confused as he takes a pair of board shorts out of his backpack and puts them on. "What's that?"

"Oh, I thought you were stripping down to prove a point."

"No." He shakes his head as he walks back over. "I know I could do it, but I've been stuck outdoors wet, cold, hungry, and God knows what else too many times to count. Enough for this lifetime and the one after it."

"I have to admit," I tell him as I run my free hand over the exposed skin just above his hip, "it's kind of hot knowing you could protect me from a bear attack, a snake bite or even a school of killer crappie fish."

Damien doesn't laugh. He looks down to where my hand is touching his skin and then raises his head slowly. "I'd do anything for you."

I want to drop the pole to the ground, stroke my hand over

every inch of him and kiss his mouth. I don't care about dinner. I don't care if I ever eat again.

He lets out a soft chuckle and moves a strand of hair behind my ear. "I like that look you get."

"Hmm?"

"Your eyes get this glazed-over look, like you're imagining something that feels *so* good."

"Yeah," I let out on a whisper.

He presses in closer, breathes out and rests his lips on that tender spot just below my ear. He cups my ass with one hand and then whispers, "Now catch us some dinner," before backing away towards the shore laughing.

Catching my breath, I complain, "I nearly dropped the damn pole. You're nothing but a tease."

"I won't be teasing you later, baby. You can count on that."

"Promises, promises," I call out, but he can't hear me. He dives underwater and doesn't resurface for what seems like forever.

"Feels great in here," he says when he finally pops back up.

"You can hold your breath for a mighty long time. A little warning would have been nice. I was just about to jump in after you."

He's treading water but I can see that he's clutching his chest. "Aw, you'd come to my rescue."

"Nope...changed my mind."

"C'mon, Gracie, take that shirt off and give me something good to look at."

"You don't deserve it."

"Tell you what...Take that shirt off and then *I'll* catch us our dinner."

"I'm perfectly capable of catching a fish."

"I just checked your line and the bait's gone. Did you feel a tug?"

"Maybe?"

He swims a few yards and then wades to the shore and comes out. "Reel it in." He goes to the truck and comes back with a big, fat worm in one hand and a fishing net in the other. He drops the net and says, "Here," as he baits the hook.

"What's with the net?"

He picks it up by the handle and runs a finger around the net's wide mouth. "This here is called insurance."

"Have some faith in me."

"I do," he says as he wades back in. "Just be careful not to hook me when you cast off, all right?"

I cast off in the polar opposite direction of Damien. Truth be told, I'm not at all confident in my abilities. And I certainly don't want to go sinking my hook into the man I'm fixing to get naked later on tonight. No, I'm not doing anything to mess that up.

Chapter Nine

## DAMIEN

I'm going to wind up carrying Grace back down the trail.

When I picked her up from her apartment this morning she was wearing the kind of sandals you'd wear to the beach. It's not like I thought she'd have a pair of good hiking boots or anything, but I did assume she'd at least have a pair of sneakers packed in her overnight bag. I suggested we skip the hike, but she was determined to see the suspension bridge I'd told her about.

"Hey, you lied to me." She turns around and nearly slips on some wet rocks.

"Be careful." I reach out to steady her as she laughs. "And what do you mean?"

She points to where some people are sitting at picnic benches outside of a small brick building. "Civilization exists, complete with working bathrooms."

I wave my hand in that direction. "By all means, take advantage of the luxury now while you still can."

"And look at those adorable log cabins!" She says as we make our way closer. "You didn't tell me about this."

"I don't know why anyone would want to stay in one of them. Might as well be in your own house. And it's way too crowded over in this section of the park."

"I do like our set-up. It feels like we're the only two people on earth where we are."

"Exactly."

Heading into the bathroom, she turns her head and says, "But running water is pretty sweet."

I don't have to go, so I spend the few minutes observing the couples and families, their campsites clustered too close together for my taste. And I can't help but smile when I focus in on a kid and his little brother. They look like they're around six and maybe four, the older one showing the other one something he's dug up from the dirt. A woman comes over, scrunching her face up but smiling when the boy shows off his slimy treasure. And it doesn't take much to imagine Grace doing just that, tending to two little boys. Our boys.

She'll make a good mother someday, warm and kind the way this woman is to her children. No, I don't believe Grace could ever be distant or demanding the way she describes her own mother.

When this woman leans down and kisses the boys, one and then the other on the tops of their heads, I suddenly feel too much emotion. My throat is tight, my eyes are stinging, and I can't pinpoint exactly why that is. But it's Grace, I know that. She brings on this tidal wave of feelings more often than I'd like to admit.

Am I thinking of her as a child, sad for her that she missed out on what those boys are getting from their mother, what I got from mine? Or am I thinking of what could be, seeing us playing the role of mom and dad in this happy little foursome, but unable to trust that a future so bright could be mine?

I want it. I want to come back and make a life with someone like Grace. I want to build a house for us, a home where we can raise our children. I want soccer practice, I want camping trips, I even want midnight feedings and dirty diapers.

A curse slips past my clenched jaw when I feel a hand on my shoulder. "You all right?"

I breathe out, letting go of the anger and regret while telling myself that everything is good, that I'll have all of that and more someday. "I'm fine. Just thinking about something I don't want to be thinking about right now."

Grace's hand makes a slow trail down from my shoulder and then rubs her thumb over mine. She gives me the opening but doesn't demand that I talk about what's troubling me, and I'm grateful for it. She just keeps hold of my hand and leans in to plant a soft kiss on my cheek when I stay quiet. "C'mon, let's head back."

We're on a secluded trail heading back to our site a few minutes later, and within those ten or so minutes Grace has slipped and fallen on her ass twice. "I am such a spaz," she says once she's upright, brushing the leaves and dirt off her backside.

"Flip flops and hiking don't mix."

"I know you don't believe me, but I did plan on packing boots. I know I took them out of my closet."

"You actually own a pair of hiking boots?"

"More like furry-lined suede boots. Probably ridiculous for this," she lifts her arms to the sides as she looks around. "But I'd give my firstborn for a pair of comfy kicks right about now."

She squeals in surprise when I pick her up and toss her over my shoulder, and then shifts to a sexy as hell purr when I run my free hand over her ass. She's laughing as my steps have her bouncing down the trail, but my heart is racing and my thoughts are heavy. I need something right now, something from her and I don't think I can wait.

I slow my steps and slide her down off my shoulder, her body brushing against mine as I lower her to the ground. Does she feel it, the state my body is in right now? I think maybe she does. I have one arm around her waist as I back her up a few steps to rest against a tree.

"Hey," I say absently, and she whispers back, "Hey what?" as her eyes drift down and over my body.

I don't answer. Don't need to. I kiss her like she's mine, dip my head down and nip her lower lip before licking and pressing my way into her mouth. When her arms come up and she laces them around my neck like she's holding on, her chest presses against mine and I let out a low moan. I don't even think it through before taking one of her hands and guiding it back down to stroke me. My hand over hers, I use her to ease the ache that's been building up to the point where now I'm damn near ready to explode.

Grace does me one better, freeing her hand to work at the button and zipper on my shorts and then slipping her hand inside so that we're skin on skin. It feels so good but I whisper, "No," knowing I'll come in her hand if she keeps this up.

She moves her hand, but only to undo the button on the little jean shorts she's wearing, then guides my hand inside and past the bikini bottoms she's got on underneath. She leans her head back against the tree and closes her eyes when I make contact, but then her hand is back on me a moment later. Kissing her and touching her as she gives the same back to me is almost as good as what I imagine fucking her will be like. She's warm and wet and rocking her hips as she moans into my mouth. Heaven.

I do come in her hand like a teenager, and she comes on mine, and after it's done I still can't stop kissing her because I've never been so devastated and wrecked by a girl in my entire life. I want to fall on my knees before her, swear that I'll give her everything just so I can have this forever. I don't even know who I am anymore, but I know I'd make a damn fool of myself for this girl without a second thought.

Breaking apart from her, I strip out of my shirt and use it to clean her hand as best I can. Grace blushes when I'm done and looks away as she buttons her shorts. But I don't want her to feel embarrassed for this, for wanting or needing. With my finger on her chin, I coax her back to me. "I'm crazy about you, Grace."

I want to tell her that I love her, because I'm pretty sure that I do, but my better sense prevails. I've been around too many lost young men, so desperate for connection that they latch on to the first girl who shows interest.

I never understood what made some of them do it, the ones who got married on the eve of a deployment. *You don't even know her*, I told Coop. *You don't know a thing about this girl.* But he did it anyway, the both of them smiling like lovesick fools in the wedding picture he stared at every night in his bunk before lights out.

I'm not a fool, I know that, but I could see myself doing some pretty stupid shit to keep the love of a woman like Grace. Maybe I'm no better than Cooper. Maybe I'm as weak as he was. I think I'm above it, that I would never crack the way he did or the way Eli almost did, but maybe I've just never been put to the test.

She pulls me back to the present whispering, "I liked that."

I imagine we're both sporting the same shy, lopsided smile when I tell her, "Yeah, me too."

Grace hops up when I gesture for her to ride piggy-back. It's another ten minutes until we're at our site, and we make the journey back in silence. Talking with Grace never feels awkward, and being quiet with her feels the same: comforting and easy.

"So, what's next on the agenda?"

"Now we get to the fun part." And right in the middle of her making some ooh-la-la sound, I add, "I'm going to show you how to clean a fish."

"Gross. And why would I need to learn how to do that?"

"It's good to have survival skills. Knowing how to start a fire, to purify water, to hunt...One of those skills could save your life someday."

"The odds of me being dropped off in the middle of nowhere and having to fend for myself are slim to none, Damien, but go ahead...Teach me."

To her credit, she doesn't flinch when I scoop the innards out with my fingers, and once I show her how to hold the knife at a forty-five degree angle, she does a decent job of separating the filet from the spine.

I hand her a plastic baggie that already has some chopped cilantro, olive oil, salt and pepper in it, and then squeeze the juice from a lime after she has the fish in there. "Massage the marinade into the fish for a minute, gently, and then I'll stick it back in the cooler."

"Massage the fish?" She shakes her head, giggling. "Changed my mind. No reality expedition show for you. You'll have a cooking show called *The Sensual Chef*. You'll film in an apron with nothing on underneath and you'll croon when you look into the camera and say, *Massage the filet, Handle the breasts with care* or," she's having a hard time catching her breath by the time she says, "*Work that meat until it's tender.*"

"Work that meat? You," I point to her, "have a dirty mind."

"My mind is all sorts of dirty when I'm around you."

"You just made my day." Stripping down to my boxers, I tell her, "Let's clean up before we start cooking. I've been dying to get back in that river all day."

Grace starts to undress but doesn't get too far. She unfastens her shorts but stops when they're halfway down over her hips. Her lips are parted and she's stuck in place.

"You all right?"

"Your body." Her eyes drift back up to meet mine. "I mean, I know you probably do conditioning drills all the time so you're in great shape, but you really are kinda...perfect."

I step closer and take the hem of her tank top. Moving it up and over her head, I fix my eyes on what I've just revealed. *She's* perfect. I run a finger over her soft skin, round and full where it peeks out from the sides of her string bikini top. Then I push her shorts down so they fall to the ground, and she steps out of them and takes my hand as I lead her down to the river.

"It's still warm," she whispers as she dips her toe into the water.

"Get on my back again. I'll walk us in so you don't have to step on the rocks."

And once we're chest deep, I let go of her so I can turn around to face her. She pops under for a moment and comes up for air, bright-eyed and smiling. "The water feels sooo good."

I've touched her everywhere, gotten to know every part of her body over the course of this month we've been together, but something about being in the water with her feels different, better. "Can I?" I ask her, touching the strings tied at the nape of her neck. She looks around. "We're alone," I reassure her. "Only I can see."

Grace nods and then her hands move to undo the strings at her back. I take the top and swim closer to the shore so I can land it on the rocks. Toss my boxers along with it. When I turn back I see she's moved in closer too. She's waist deep now, so her tits are on full display just for me.

"You," I tell her, "you're the one who's perfect."

She lets me. She lets me cup her breasts, press them together so that I can feel and lick and suck them. She lets me slip her out of her bottoms, lets me cup her ass and inch my fingers in close. And she guides me closer, wrapping her legs around my waist so that she can feel me hard and pressing against her. She knows I want her again and I know she wants me.

There's just a bit of orange purple pink left in the sky. It will be night before long.

"I've never gone skinny dipping before," she says with her arms laced around my neck. "I'm definitely a fan."

"It makes you want to build a house right next to a lake, a river or a beach, doesn't it?" I look back to the bank where our makeshift home for the night is set up. "We could do this every day."

"Neighbors might think we're a little wonky."

"Nah, they'd just be jealous."

"We'd meet up after work, catch us some crappie—"

"You'd skin it since you're an expert now."

"I am." She smiles proudly. "And an expert skinny dipper, too."

"That you are, woman."

Grace takes one of my hands from where it's resting behind her back and guides it to where we're pressed up against each other. Her eyes flutter closed when I touch her, and I swear, it's the most beautiful sight I've ever seen. "So fucking hot," I whisper before telling her to hold on tight.

It's been this unspoken thing between us, when it's going to happen. I'm with her nearly every single day at some point, and we haven't exactly been keeping things chaste. But I've held back even when she's made it clear she wanted me to keep going. I don't see her as a hook up and I don't want her to feel used the way she did before. I'm leaving. And while that doesn't mean sex is off the table, it does make it somewhat more complicated. It's like Grace has *handle with care* stamped all over her body.

"I, um, came prepared," she tells me as we reach the bank.

I stop and kiss her once before setting her back on solid ground. "You did?"

She nods before going to get our wet things from the rocks. I follow, take what she's holding and tell her, "Don't get dressed." And I feel like Adam and Eve walking the short distance between the river and our tent, out in the open, naked as the Lord made us. It feels like we're the only two people on this earth right now, and I'm more than fine with that.

She scoots back, holding her knees to her chest once we're inside and she's settled on the sleeping bags that cover the tent floor. "I'm not on the pill or anything. I just figured it wasn't worth it being that you're leaving so soon. But I did bring—"

I finish the sentence for her. "I did too." Her eyes are fixed on my dick as I go to get the condoms from my bag, but I ask her anyway, "Are you sure?"

"I've *been* sure."

Grace unwraps her arms from around her knees slowly, props her hands on the floor behind her and parts her knees just the slightest bit. It's her way of telling me that she's mine for the taking.

I ease her knees further apart so I can taste her. Long, slow licks that leave her gasping and clutching the blanket beneath her. I look up, wanting to catch even the slightest movement, and I'm rewarded by the sight of her tits and the lustful look in her eyes.

She tells me she wants my cock, whispering the words as she circles her hips against my mouth. But I want to make her come, want to sink inside of her right at that moment when she topples off the cliff. Here eyes are back on me, hungry as I roll the condom on, and she spreads her legs again to welcome me inside. It doesn't take long, touching her until she can't hold out, and I push inside as her muscles contract around me. Fuck, fuck, fuck—I never want to stop. She responds, whispers *yes*, and moves the way you dream that a woman will. Her hands are on my ass, pulling me in deeper, and she's begging me to make her come again. And when she does, I follow. I am wrung out and bone tired in the best possible way, moving her to rest at my side once I roll onto my back.

"I'm pretty sure it doesn't get any better than that." She doesn't say anything in return, and when I look down I can see that she's troubled. I'm not a manwhore, not into the fuck buddy thing, but I'm experienced and I've never had any complaints before. "Was it good for you?"

"Oh. Yeah, of course."

"Hey," I turn her chin up so she's looking at me, "where'd you go just now?"

She looks like she's bracing for impact when she asks, "Does it bother you? Like, when I spoke that way during sex...Is it too much?"

"What do you mean?"

"I think maybe I get a little carried away."

"Why is that a bad thing?"

"You don't think I sounded like a..."

"What?"

"Like a slut?"

I turn onto my side so we're face to face. "No! Everything you did, everything you said...I loved it."

She nods her head once, forces a smile. "Good."

"I've gotta ask...What would make you think that?"

Grace breathes in deep. "I kind of went through the rest of my high school years thinking I was a slut, even though I was never with anyone in that way after Peter."

"Why?"

"I come from a buttoned-up, traditional kind of town. Pretty sure I was the only girl in the freshman class having sex." She bites her lip before adding, "Sex on a regular basis and, um, liking it, too."

"And then when he did that to you..."

"I felt really, really stupid."

"But you're not. You weren't back then either."

She's quiet for a moment before meeting my eyes again. "Have I ruined this? I mean, have I ruined tonight by bringing all of that garbage from my past up again?"

"Never. And I'll never judge you. You know that, right?" She nods and I kiss her head.

She moves to straddle me, bracing her hands on my chest. "So now you know me, Damien, warts and all."

And I see the back and forth, the conflict in her eyes. Trying to smile her way through something that still hurts. She's young. Not even twenty years old and still just trying to figure it all out like the rest of us.

My eyes rake over her. She's perfect but I know she can't

see herself through my eyes. Grace likes her body but doesn't always like the attention it attracts, she likes sex but she's ashamed of liking it, she wants to be a woman but still thinks she needs permission to be one.

I run my hands down her back and then up again, pulling her close to rest her chest against mine. "Never in a million years, Grace...I never thought I'd meet someone who makes me feel the way you do."

"Same here," she whispers into my skin.

And we spend the rest of the night building a fire, cooking together, eating fish and drinking a few beers, and it's safe to say that I've never been happier in my life.

Chapter Ten

GRACE

This is what it's supposed to be like.

I may have been naïve back in high school, but I was never a blind fool. I knew the fact that Peter never acknowledged me in public meant something. Passing him in the crowded hallways, he went on joking with his friends or acting like he was preoccupied in some way, never meeting my eyes. I was instructed to wait for him on a corner a few blocks away from our high school instead of meeting him by his car in the student parking lot after class. And when I'd get in, I'd watch as his eyes scanned the area. He didn't want to be spotted with me, that was clear. And I thought so little of myself back then that I let him get away with it. I was on board with being nothing more than some boy's dirty little secret.

It's so different now. Damien makes me feel special and adored. He holds my hand, carries my bag when he meets me on campus, opens doors for me. When we're out with Eli and their other friends, Damien thinks nothing of wrapping an arm around my shoulder or pulling me onto his lap. He wants to tell the world that I'm his.

It's not like I was some cowering wallflower before he came onto the scene, but his attention makes me walk taller.

He's been in my bed just about every night since our camping trip. I can't get enough, and I think the same goes for him. But it's not just the act itself, and how physically good he makes me feel. Still naked and curled up beside him, it's what passes between us after that makes me feel close to him. More often than not he's gone in the morning by the time I wake up, but the hours spent talking in the dark before I fall asleep are sacred and ours alone.

He's careful when he talks about the future. He'll tell me something and then pop a subtle question like: *Can you see yourself staying in North Carolina after you graduate?* Questions that make me smile. Does he see me as a part of the life he's mapping out for himself once his next tour is done? I hope so, but don't come right out with it. We've only known each other for one month as of tomorrow, so professing my love would be ridiculous, and something I'm too cautious to do. I think he feels the same.

*Yes*, I told him, *I can see myself staying in the Carolinas*. I do love the weather and I love the area. And once I drop the bomb about my change in career plans to my parents, I don't see myself moving back home to Pennsylvania, so I'm going to have to get a job teaching right away and find an apartment. *You can stay there with me whenever you're home on leave*, I want to tell him, but I don't.

"Any chance you'll be home for Christmas?" I ask him tonight.

Damien laughs before kissing the top of my head. "Not likely. When I do get to come back stateside it's not usually for holidays. It's on short notice and I never know for how long...Could be for three days or three weeks. We never get much in terms of advance notice."

"Will you tell me when you're coming back?"

He pauses before asking, "Do you want me to?"

I nod knowing that he can feel it against his chest. "I want to see you." The words hang in the air for a moment before I back-peddle. "I mean, if that's what *you* want."

"I want you. That's not up for debate, Grace. And if I had my way, I'd keep you boxed up and waiting for me until I get home, but I can't do that. I won't have you putting your life on hold for me."

His words make me feel hopeful and deflated at once. He wants me, he says, but he's also not committing to anything, not putting either of our lives *on hold*.

I'm sulking when I tell him, "My life isn't all that exciting," because I'd gladly put my life on hold for him. I'd wait for him if he'd only ask.

He shifts on the bed so we're face to face. "You're still in college. You should experience all of this...your friends, the parties, everything. You should be free to," he takes a breath, "meet other people."

I bite my lip to keep from showing him how much those words hurt. I don't want to meet anyone else, but maybe he does.

"You might meet someone over there," I whisper, and he shakes his head and laughs like I've said something absurd. He's on his back now, looking up at the ceiling, and I'd give anything to know what's running through his mind. "Is that so crazy? You could meet another soldier, or a civilian woman from the country where you're stationed. Hey, I know it happens. *The Notebook* is one of my favorite movies."

"I don't follow."

"You could fall in love with the nurse who cares for you, you might have some gorgeous commanding officer this time around, or maybe you'll rescue a woman and she'll get some hero worship complex for you."

He shuts me up with a kiss. "You watch too many movies." Running a hand through my hair he says, "And you might meet someone here...Someone who can be with you day in and day out. Maybe I'll be the one getting a *Dear John* letter."

I close my eyes. "That was a sad one. Nicholas Sparks gets me every time."

"I actually saw that one, too."

"Did you cry?"

He looks at me like I'm high but then cracks a smile. "Maybe my eyes got a little misty."

"So all this talk, this is you trying to protect both of us?"

"Maybe I want to protect you from me." But before I can ask why, he changes the subject. "My life over there isn't half as dramatic, or even the slightest bit romantic the way you imagine it."

"What's it like?"

"It's a lot of things. It's a hurry up and wait situation most of the time, so there can be long stretches of time that are tedious and boring. Then just when you start getting used to some semblance of peace, everything is turned upside down by some really violent and stressful shit." He sighs and rolls onto his back again. This time I follow, draping my body over his chest, and I'm comforted by the feel of his hand slowly coasting up and down over my back. "Some of the men do get caught up in the hero worship thing, though. You did get that part right."

"I could see that."

"You're dropped in these miserable places, where just about everyone is poor by our standards, and they're struggling. We come in. We wreck everything first and then build it back up, or we try to anyway. It's crazy and it's backwards, but giving those people something as basic as fresh water is monumental. Water, can you imagine that?"

"And I imagine they're grateful."

"Some see you as a savior, some see you as the source of their misery." He lets out a cheerless laugh. "People back here have no idea what it's like. They watch the news footage and think they know but they don't. I've heard people refer to them as savages, uneducated and primitive. Like we're somehow morally superior. One thing this war has taught me is that we're all the same. They love their families, they dream and hope for a good life just like we do, but when hard pressed, people do what they have to do to survive."

"I can't imagine living in a war-torn region."

"We take a lot of things for granted."

"There's this theory I'm learning about in my Child Development class. It's called the Hierarchy of Needs."

"Maslow."

"How do you know that, smarty pants? Weren't you a finance major?"

"He's New York City, born and bred."

"I didn't know that."

"Yep, Brooklyn. My mother wasn't educated but she was well-read. I'd always pick up whatever she was reading. Everything I know about art, politics and philosophy is because of her."

"She sounds like an interesting woman."

"She was. She didn't get a chance to go to college, and in her case that was a real shame."

"Where was she originally from?"

"She was born here but her parents were from Ireland."

"And your father?"

"Norway. He came over here with his older brother, my namesake, when he was fourteen."

"That must have been hard."

"He never complained, but I'm sure it was." He turns to me and smiles. "Your boy Maslow would say that sitting around pondering what you're missing out on is a luxury to people who are trying to keep a roof over their heads and food on the table."

"Yes. And I'm sure that some of the people you've met have made some terrible choices, but they're just trying to stay alive."

"Exactly."

"Why did you reenlist?"

"If you asked me a few months ago I would have been able to tell you, but right now I'm not so sure. When I made the decision we were coming off what I considered to be a big victory."

"In battle?"

"No." He shakes head. "We spent the last eighteen months in some shit hole about an hour outside of Bagdad. We were tasked with providing a water system to a village after the place had been bombed and we'd completely destroyed their infrastructure. There were battles on and off, with insurgents trying to disrupt the work we were doing, but it wasn't large scale like when I first got there."

"But it was dangerous?"

"Every day is dangerous. You don't know if the villager giving you intel is walking you into a trap, or if the kid asking you for a piece of gum just finished helping his brother plant

IEDs along the roadside. And that kid doesn't know if he's going to make it back across the street without a stray bullet hitting him. It's fucked over there."

"So what happened that made you reenlist?"

"We were in the middle of a bad stretch...Constant bullshit, sniper attacks. One of the men in our unit had both his legs blown off one week, the next week one killed himself after getting dumped by his wife. And when I say men, I'm referring to a nineteen-year-old and a twenty-year-old. So make that boys, not men.

"Cooper, the guy who shot himself? He was a good friend of Eli's and a good friend of mine. We were in his wedding party." His body tenses beneath mine. "Ridiculous... It was two days before we shipped out to some girl he barely knew."

"And he was so broken up over it that he killed himself?"

"It was a clusterfuck kind of a week and her letter was the cherry on top of a crap sundae. He just broke."

"I'm so sorry."

"The day before he killed himself we got assigned to disrupt a group that had been smuggling weapons. We didn't suffer any casualties but they did. And when we went to inspect their trucks, instead of finding guns we found girls." I look up at him. "Some as young as ten, locked in the back like cattle on their way to a nearby Taliban camp."

"Trafficked?"

He nods. "They were dirty, scared, and you could see...Most of them had already been assaulted."

"Raped."

"Yes."

I sit up on the bed, feeling sick to my stomach. "Ten years old. Were they kidnapped?"

"Some were, but some of them were traded. Desperate people do desperate things."

"Oh my God."

He gently pulls me back down to rest on his chest. "But I saw it as a huge victory. We saved them, right? I imagined them being sent off to Europe or to the states, going to school, on the path to a better life. And maybe I was being a little pie in the sky about the whole thing, but Eli and a few of the others saw that day as a final confirmation of how fruitless our efforts were over there. That we were doomed, same as those girls, and nothing would ever change."

"How do you see it now?"

"I don't feel as strong in my convictions as I used to. I don't know if we're helping those people or if they even want our help. I still believe I'm defending something worthwhile, but I'd be lying if I told you I'm still a true blue patriot."

"Questioning your purpose doesn't make you unpatriotic."

"I know." Damien situates me so that I'm resting on top of him chin to toes. "I'm just feeling sorry for myself. Going to miss this when I'm gone. I'm going to miss you, Grace."

I dig deep and muster up some courage. "What I said before?"

"What?"

"I *do* want to see you when you come home," I tell him. "Promise me, ok?"

He rubs his nose against mine and whispers, "I promise."

# Chapter Eleven

## DAMIEN

This girl sleeps like the dead.

I smile to myself as I ease out of the bed, and then look down at her sleeping peacefully as I dress. She doesn't stir. Her sleep is deep and sound. I envy her that.

I don't think I've had a good night's sleep in years. Not since my mother got sick. Since then I've always had something or someone to worry about. If it wasn't my mother it was my father, then it was the men in my unit and now it's Eli in particular. And I worry about Grace.

She's not in danger but I worry about her nonetheless. I worry that she'll get mugged walking home from the library late at night, or get attacked coming home from a bar even though she lives in a relatively safe community. I worry that she won't be able to defend herself when I'm not around. It's a baseless fear, I know that, but I've been conditioned to expect the worst.

I scribble out a note and leave it next to her phone on the

nightstand. *Come camping with me Saturday?* I want to relive that last trip as many times as I can before I leave. She'll say yes, I know she will. It makes me unsettled to think of her in that way, obedient and seeking to please, but I've noticed the tendency she has to bend to the will of others. It's how that kid Peter got her to do his bidding.

The sound of my keys scraping along the table as I pick them up rouses her. "Where are you going?" she asks in a sleepy voice.

"Heading out. I want you to get a good sleep."

She rubs at her eyes and then focuses on me. "I sleep best when you're here with me." And now I'm thinking that maybe I've gotten it all wrong. Maybe she's got me bending to her will when she arches just slightly so that the sheet moves down and reveals the tops of her breasts. She runs one hand up and over herself while I can see the outline of her other hand moving south beneath the sheet. Her eyes are still on mine when she lets out a soft *ah,* and then her eyes rake down my body. "Don't leave. I want you to fuck me again, Damien."

I pull at the sheet so I can watch her touch herself. The inside of my mouth gets wet watching her hand move between her legs. And I don't know where to go first once I'm back out of my clothes, her mouth, her ass, the heavy swell of her breasts. I want to maul and rut and fuck, want to take her every way. I just barely remember to grab a condom from her nightstand before lining myself up and pushing inside of her. I feel like she was made just for me. The soft sounds she makes when I hit her deep, the dirty, sexy words she whispers to urge me on, the way I fit inside of her just so.

"I love you," I whisper as I come down from the high.

She rakes her nails down and over my back. "I love you too."

I've never said it before and neither has she, but I've felt it for some time. And it's all right. I want her to know. I'd never want to leave without her knowing just how special she is to me.

I look at her as I pull out and ease back. "You ok?"

"Yeah," she answers, but her smile is sad. "I'm just thinking about the end already, and I don't want this to end."

"It doesn't have to end." I tell her this, going against my better judgement. But fuck it, I do want to bind Grace to me. I want her waiting for me to come home. I want her thinking about the future that I've pretty much mapped out for us.

I let what I've said hang in the air while I go into the bathroom to dispose of the condom. When I come back out, Grace is propped up on her elbow, naked again from the waist up, patting the space next to her on the bed.

Fixing my eyes on her breasts I tell her, "You are the hottest woman on the planet, you know that?"

"Stop." She's smiling and cringing at the same time, still uncomfortable when I compliment her.

I ease back onto the bed and lay down so that I'm facing her. "I meant what I said, Grace. I love you." When she doesn't answer I decide to put it all out there. "If you ever did decide to wait for me, I'd make a good life for us. Eli and I have plans. He's an engineering major, and I've got experience with the construction side and some knowledge of finance. We're going into business together when I get out. We'll be taking over for his father someday. I'll be making good money, Grace."

She blushes and shakes her head. "I don't care about that."

"But I do. I don't want to scare you off or anything, but I can see my future here with you."

I let out the breath I've been holding when I see that Grace looks happy. "A house right by the river?" she asks.

I nod, picturing it. "With a wraparound deck and some steps that lead right down to the water."

"Easy access for skinny dipping?"

"That's a must."

"I want a fire pit, too." She reaches over me to grab the note off the nightstand. Handing it to me she says, "Bring stuff to make s'mores this weekend."

"No problem. This weekend we're breaking all the rules."

"You mean the hunt, catch and kill rules don't apply?"

"I'm thinking I'll marinate some steaks, and I'll pack eggs and bacon to make on the cast iron pan for breakfast Sunday morning."

"I'll make a caprese salad to go with the steaks and I'll bust out the bottle of Prosecco I've got chilling in the fridge."

"Yeah," I kiss her once, "we'll make this last camping trip a good one."

My words hang in the air.

Last.

I hate the word when I think of it as an adjective. It's final, an ending, something coming to its conclusion. I like the verb much better. As in, I want this goodness to last. I want to hang on, to endure, to go the distance with Grace.

I'm pretty sure she's thinking along the same lines I am, but she chooses to lighten the mood. Her hand skims along my hip and then grazes my dick when he says, "You better bring you're A-game this weekend."

I laugh even though it feels like there's a rock lodged in my chest. "I always do, don't I?"

"You don't hear this girl complaining."

I kiss her so she can't get a good look at my face. It's getting too hard to hide from her and I don't want our last few days together to be sad ones.

# Chapter Twelve

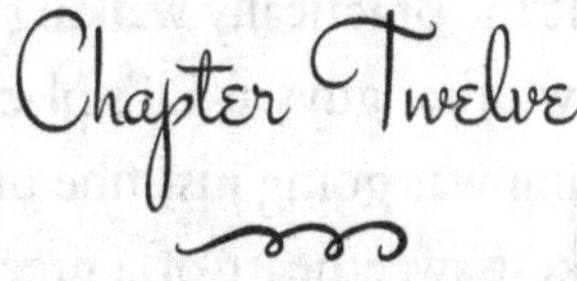

GRACE

One week. That's all we have left.

I'm trying my best and so is he, but it's weighing on the both of us. A dark cloud that descends right after you laugh or you kiss or you smile. An ominous voice inside of your head reminding you at every turn, *Don't get used to this.*

And he's bailed on me twice this week. Once because Eli was drunk at a friend's house while insisting he was fine to drive home, and once because Eli's father was short-handed at a worksite and needed extra help to meet a deadline.

Gianna called Damien to come to the rescue the other night. She calls, he jumps. It's not really like that, I'm being petty, but I do get the feeling the girl would do anything in her power to come between us. I saw the way she looked at him that first night. She wanted him for herself—still does.

I was over at Eli's apartment with Damien last Monday night to watch football. I was still riding the high I was on from our weekend camping trip. It was too cold to swim this time, so no naughty skinny dipping at night, but it was amazing and mind-blowing and so special. Lying in his arms that night, I realized that I've never once felt this way before because Damien makes me feel cherished and adored. It's a heady feeling, and one that left me practically walking on air.

There were a few other guys at Eli's place, one with his girlfriend, and everything was going just fine until she showed up. She gave me the fakest sweetheart of a greeting when Damien was in the room, but then shot me a look like I was crap stuck to the bottom of her shoe once his back was turned.

I was sitting there, seething with a smile on my face when she sat down on the couch and basically ordered him to fetch her a drink, making a show of saying, "You pick...You know what I like," when he asked what kind of beer she wanted.

Damien seems oblivious to her manipulative bullshit, and I won't lower myself to whine about it. I won't give her the satisfaction. I did have Frannie pick me up early from Eli's, giving Damien some lame excuse about needing to study when I didn't, but that's as far as it's gone.

When we're together I don't want that girl anywhere near, don't want to hear her name, don't want to waste what little time we have left even thinking about her.

*And here we go again*, I tell myself when Damien's phone vibrates. He picks it up, looks at the screen and then turns it over before putting it back on my nightstand. The buzzing stops and then starts up again not two minutes later.

"Should you get that?"

He shakes his head and then sighs a moment later. The phone is rattling over the surface of the table, impossible to ignore.

Damien's words are clipped when he answers, "What's up?" and then he's pinching the bridge of his nose with his free hand. "No, I can't come right now. I'll text him but I'm sure he's fine." He pauses and then repeats, "I'm sure he's fine. I'll call you back."

He lets out a breath and gives me an absent *sorry* as he shoots off a text. It must be to Eli. And it was a girl's voice on the other end of the line just now, so I'm sure it was Gianna calling.

A caring person would ask if everything is all right, but I'm feeling way more passive aggressive than compassionate right now. I sit up and put the shirt Damien just peeled off me back on. I can feel his eyes on me as I get up and go to the kitchen for some water.

I'm staring ahead at nothing when I feel him come up behind me and kiss the top of my head. "I'm sorry about that."

"Why does she do that?" I'm so angry I can barely get the words out.

"What do you mean?"

I step away from him. The boy isn't stupid, and I'm running low on patience at the moment. "Did you two have something together?" When he doesn't answer I turn to face him. "Gianna is a little territorial when it comes to you, wouldn't you say?" I dump the rest of my water into the sink. "It's ridiculous the way she calls you all the time and just expects you to drop everything."

And when I say drop everything, I'm referring to me. She wants him to drop *me*.

"It's because of Eli."

"And is Eli all right? Were you able to get in touch with him?"

"He's out with a few of the guys he met from the rugby club. He's fine but I might swing by the bar on my way home just to make sure."

"Right. And I guess you're on your way home now?" I sound like a witch.

"Grace." He says my name like a plea.

I walk to the door and open it for him, all the while reminding myself of what I swore just moments before: *I won't give her the satisfaction.* But it's hard and I'm angry and that nagging voice in my head won't shut up.

"You didn't answer my question."

He's still standing in the kitchen even though the front door is now wide open and I'm basically kicking him out.

I can't stop this. Can't stem the tide of my hatred for Gianna. Can't help but feel jealous and helpless. And I'm mad at myself, too. We have just a few days left and I'm fucking this up. *She's fucking this up*, my inner nasty witch reminds me.

"Did you have something with G?" I practically spit that one letter, hating him for having a stupid nickname for that girl.

He takes his leather jacket off the couch and puts it on, looking tired and defeated. "I kissed her once, a long time ago." He doesn't even meet my eyes as he walks out the door adding, "And I've regretted it every day since."

# Chapter Thirteen

DAMIEN

The sun is just coming up when I hear Eli bang into the wall on his way to the bathroom. I'm grateful that he at least woke up rather than pissing the bed until I hear the heavy stream of urine hitting off the tiles. He missed the toilet entirely—again. Last time he did that I walked into the bathroom barefoot the next morning and stepped in it.

Fucking idiot.

He's getting worse, not better.

He's angry at his professors, at the comments his fellow students make in class, angry at the state of the world in general. He's angry at me, at his parents, at the way that stranger looked at him in the bar last night.

When I got there his new friends were holding him back. He apparently jumped some guy who'd accidentally bumped into him, and then proceeded to beat the shit out of him right in front of his girl.

The guy from his history class who'd invited him to check

out the rugby club not so subtly let me know that it wasn't going to work out. And if a bunch of guys who play a violent, physically punishing game don't want you around, you know something's seriously wrong.

I'm going to speak to his father today. I'm leaving next week and I don't feel good about it. I know I deserve a life, I deserve to have Grace, but I also know I've done a piss poor job of keeping my best friend on the straight and narrow. He needs more than the weekly therapy sessions he's been getting. He needs to stop drinking, to be in a twelve-step program, to be in a veteran's support group or something. He needs more help.

This leave was supposed to be about helping Eli, but I've spent most of my time stateside laser focused on Grace. So I'm fucking up where Eli is concerned, and Grace made it clear last night that I'm fucking up where she's concerned, too.

The look on her face when she basically showed me the door crushed me. She was some mixed-up combination of jealous, resentful and hurt. She's a smart girl, so I know she doesn't really believe I have feelings for anyone except her, but putting myself in Grace's shoes, I can't say I would have reacted any better.

Gianna's timing sucks. Her calls always come in when Grace and I are in the middle of something good. And by something good, I'm not just referring to sex. She interrupts that too, but I find it more irritating when Gianna crashes those moments when Grace and I are just talking, or when I'm holding her while we're watching a movie in bed.

I'm about to suggest that Eli drink some water as he exits the bathroom, but that would be enabling his drunk ass and I won't do it. He deserves the hangover he'll be suffering through today. We're both due at his father's work site in two hours, and I imagine the sounds of saws buzzing and jackhammers breaking ground won't make Eli's day all too pleasant. Serves him right.

He's more than halfway through his first semester. He's intelligent, so he's been muddling through even though he's not giving it his all, but he's taking mostly core curriculum classes now like English Lit, History and Humanities. Once his engineering classes kick into high gear, he's going to shit the bed if he doesn't change his ways. There's no way he can pass those classes with the half-assed effort he's been giving. It's safe to say he wouldn't even be getting out of bed and going to classes if I wasn't here nagging him every morning.

I'm beat. Barely got any sleep after I dragged him home last night. I'm worried about Eli—seriously worried—and I can't stop thinking about Grace either. Time is a precious commodity, and I've got very little of it left. Six days until I head back to base, and then maybe a few days or a week until I'm back on a plane and heading off to God knows where.

She's going to move on, to forget me. I thought maybe I had a shot at planting a seed and making something lasting out of what we have, but this week has put that future into question.

I want to call her right now and apologize again, promise her I'll see her tonight and that nothing will come between us, but I know I'm starting to sound like a broken record, let alone a liar. Fact is, if Eli needs me I'll be there.

I won't leave him twisting in the wind the way I left Cooper.

I'm grateful for the knock on the door that interrupts another stroll down memory lane—make that *worst* memory lane—but then my mood darkens when I hear the key turn in the lock before I can get up to answer it. The only person who knocks once and then uses her key is Gianna.

"Hey." Her voice is soft as she surveys the place for damage.

"Eli didn't put up a fight...Not with me, anyway."

"Was it bad? My friend Keith was at the bar and told me that," she lowers her voice to a whisper, "Eli was acting like an absolute dick."

"Maybe he needs to hear that, G. Everyone treats him with kid gloves. You, your parents...I'm guilty of it too. He needs to know he's fucking up, needs to be held accountable."

She lowers herself to sit across from me on the floor. "Tough love? We tried that approach when he first got home and wrecked my father's truck."

I don't want or need the reminder. Wreck the truck? Eli was trying to plow head-on into a tree. That was attempt number two. "Sorry. I know this hasn't been easy on you."

"I thought he was doing great a few months ago. When you came to stay, he was definitely starting to turn it around. Now he's taking two steps back for every step forward."

Her words hit their mark. "You think I'm not doing enough for him?"

"I didn't say that, Damien."

"But it's what you're thinking." I gesture for her to turn her head so I can stand up and pull on my jeans from the night before. "It's what I'm thinking, too."

Her gaze travels over my body before she meets my eyes again. I'm not vain, don't think I'm God's gift to women or anything, but I'm wishing I had a shirt handy to cover myself right now because she's eyeing me like I'm her very own dirty fantasy come to life. I head towards the kitchen, looking around, but then remember that my shirt from last night is in the trash, stained with that poor guy's blood after I helped him back to his car and begged him not to press charges against Eli.

"I'm just asking, is she worth it?"

I'm glad Gianna can't see my face right now because my eyes are daggers. Fuck you, fuck him, fuck all of this. *I'm one person*, I want to tell them. *I'm not some superhero who can magically cure Eli.*

I take my time measuring out the coffee, and say nothing as the machine hisses and the pot fills. A few quiet minutes pass before I turn back to her and say, "I'm in love with Grace."

I want to be clear, leave no doubt on where it is that I stand, but maybe I also want to wound Gianna. And once the words are out of my mouth, I know I've succeeded in doing at least one thing today.

I expect her to say something mean, to mask her hurt and hit me back, but she doesn't. She looks away and then turns back a moment later. "What is it about me?" When I don't answer, she presses, "What is it? Men like me for a night, a few weeks tops, but then they move on. I just want to know why."

*Fuck.*

Nasty Gianna is easier to deal with. I can hate her, blame her for the desperate sadness that's filling me when I think about how little time I have left with Grace. But this girl in front of me now? She's Gianna at seventeen: clueless and earnest and lost.

"You're a good person. I see that whenever you're around Eli. You're caring, you're thoughtful…"

"But?"

"You're not so nice to people you don't know, and you act like people are beneath you sometimes."

"Is that what Grace says about me?"

"Honestly, she doesn't talk about you at all." That's a lie, but I'm not about to drag Grace into this. "It's what I see. The night you met her is a good example, though. You were mean to her for no reason."

"I didn't know that was you! All I saw was some girl letting a guy feel her up in the middle of the bar!"

I sip my coffee, give myself a moment, because it's hard to keep my voice low and even when I respond to that bullshit. "First off, I wasn't feeling her up...That's ridiculous. And second, you just proved my point. It shouldn't have mattered if she was with me or not. You were rude, plain and simple, and you tried your best to make her feel like shit."

"I apologized."

"A half-assed apology."

She stews on that for a minute before whispering, "I didn't like it."

"What?"

She swallows and then meets my eyes. "I didn't like watching you kiss her."

I shake my head, knowing where this is going. "Gianna..."

She stands and makes her way over until she's standing less than a foot in front of me. "I wanted it to be me. I wanted you to be kissing me again."

"That was a lifetime ago."

"Maybe for you," she places her palm over my bare chest, "but I still think about it all the time."

"It was a mistake."

She backs up a step, her features hardening into the face that's more familiar. "A mistake? And don't give me that *I'm too old for you* bullshit because I'm the same age as her."

"You were too young back then. I was wrong to kiss you that night."

"And now you just don't—"

"I don't see you that way."

She looks down at herself, at the tight jeans that mold to

her every curve and the fitted shirt that's got one button too many undone. "Every man sees me that way."

She doesn't get it. She never did. "You're more than that, G."

Gianna shakes her head. "If that was true then you'd give this a chance."

"It doesn't work like that. Sometimes you're just drawn to someone, like it's beyond your control."

"And you're drawn to Grace...Plain, quiet as a mouse Grace."

Now I'm amused. Grace is anything but quiet, and she sure as shit isn't plain. She's beautiful and Gianna knows it.

"Plain? Quiet as a mouse? I thought you said she was a party girl, the queen of fraternity row." Gianna's face falls, and in that split second I go from being annoyed with her to feeling shitty for teasing her. "Hey," I take one step closer and touch her cheek, "I'm sorry."

Her eyes are pleading as she moves in closer and puts her hand over mine. "I'll wait for you. She won't." When I go to move my hand away she grips it. "My family loves you and *I* love you, Damien. We could make a life together here." I'm shaking my head when she says, "I'll make you happy, I swear."

I know it's going to come out sounding wrong before I even say it, but the words are out of my mouth before I can stop. "Someday you're going to meet someone. You'll love him and he's going to worship the ground you walk on."

Her hand falls back down to her side. "Thanks."

"Gianna."

She looks around and then walks over to the coffee table when she spots her keys. "No really, thank you for letting me down easy, asshole."

There's nothing I can say to make this better, so I keep my trap shut.

"My mother expects you and Eli for dinner tonight, but whatever, you do you."

"What's that supposed to mean?"

"It means you've made it pretty clear to everyone that being with her is your top priority."

"That's bullshit."

With her hand on the doorknob she looks down the hallway towards Eli's bedroom. "Is it?"

She's gone before I can argue, not that I have anything to say in my defense.

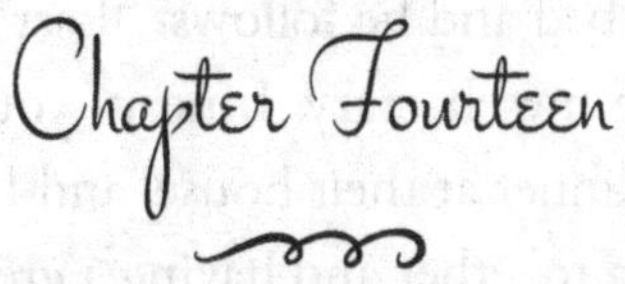

# Chapter Fourteen

**GRACE**

"Can I come in?"

Damien looks bone tired. I stand back to let him pass, feeling miserable over the way I've acted. I set out to punish him for this allegiance he has to Gianna, imagined or not, and just one look at his face tells me I've succeeded.

"You haven't answered my calls."

"I thought I'd say something I'd regret if I did, so..."

"So you just decided to blow me off?"

I cross my arms, digging in, but then remind myself that there's no satisfaction in winning when I'm fighting with Damien. My arms fall back to my sides as I gesture for him to follow me into my room.

"I don't like this feeling."

"What are you saying, exactly?"

"I hate myself for being jealous, for being angry, and I hate that I'm taking it out on you."

"If the roles were reversed, I'd be angry too, but you have to know that there's nothing between me and Gianna. I think you do know that."

"I believe you, if that's what you're asking me. But I know she has feelings for you, and I'm not comfortable with that." I take a seat on my bed and he follows. "Last night I was sitting here alone driving myself crazy. I mean, you texted to tell me you were having dinner at their house, and I was just picturing all of you laughing together and having a great time." I put my hand on his knee to stop him before he can respond. "You're tied to her in a way that's different. We're new and what we have is fragile, while you're practically a part of her family, her brother's best friend. It's cozy and familiar in a way that we're just...not."

"I see her as just that, my best friend's sister, nothing more."

"But when it comes to helping Eli, you two are, I don't know...Like a team. I get it, but it still doesn't make it easy to handle when she calls and you go running."

He takes my hand, rubbing his thumb over it to soothe me as we sit in silence.

"Hey, look at me." I'm trying my best not to cry but it's no use. I cough to clear my throat and look down into my lap so I can bat away the errant tears. But he turns my chin so I have no choice but to face him, and then kisses one cheek and then the other, taking my tears as his own. "I should have filled you in better. That's on me."

"What do you mean?"

"Eli tried to kill himself right at the end of our tour."

"Right after your friend?"

"Cooper, yeah." He pauses for a full minute, and I wait so he can work out whatever it is that he's trying to tell me. "The last few months of that tour were a struggle for every single one of us, but Eli and a few of the others just fell into a black hole or something. Coop never made it home," he pauses to clear his throat, "but for the others, you'd think coming home would make the depression or trauma or whatever it is ease up some. I mean, you're back, you're outta there. But it's like it gets worse. It's like me and everyone else around Eli has to remind him day after day after day that he's got something to live for."

"He doesn't see it that way?"

"He's having a hard time adjusting to civilian life. He doesn't know who he is outside of being a Marine, and truth is, he wasn't all that gung-ho about being a Marine in the first place. He's just lost. All that stuff about Eli and me going into business with his dad when he finishes school and I get out? That's me and Mr. Oliveri hatching those plans. Eli is ambivalent."

"How are the others?"

"Most of us are doing all right, but two of the guys from our platoon are struggling like Eli. They're in and out of the VA hospital, getting prescribed whatever meds they can get their hands on. I'm not a doctor so I don't know jack shit, but I don't think those pills do much of anything besides get you hooked on pills."

"They aren't in therapy?"

"Eli is but I don't know about the others. And you do need therapy, along with family and friends around you, but most of all you need a purpose."

"A purpose?"

"A belief that you have something to contribute, that you have a future, or maybe it's just knowing you have people who are counting on you."

"Eli has all of that, doesn't he?"

"He has the support of family and friends, he's in therapy twice a week, but a purpose? No, I don't think he's bought into the idea of his future. Not yet, anyway."

"It would be nice if he met someone."

"She'd have to be someone pretty special. He's a lot to take on at the moment. But I've had the same thought myself." He squeezes my hand gently. "Talking to you, or just being with you even when we're not talking? I know for a fact that it helps me."

"It does?"

His expression is somber when he nods. "You make me happy, Grace. You make me think I've got a future that's worth fighting for, a person and a life to come home to. And that's not me using words to trap you in place or guilt you into staying with me. I understand that time and distance can wreck what we have, and believe me, I am so angry at myself. I don't want to leave you. But falling in love with you has me believing that maybe someday I can have that life...You, me, a house right on the river. And even if I don't get to have that with you, I'd still be grateful for what you've given me these past few weeks."

"I can't stomach the thought of you leaving, even though I know we only have a few days left."

"I keep telling myself not to focus on that, to enjoy every minute I still have left here, but that's just well-intentioned bullshit."

"But it's the only thing we can do. I don't want to spend the next couple of days crying over the fact that you're leaving. I'll have plenty of time for crying after you're gone." I turn his chin so he's looking right at me. "As of tomorrow we have five days left. Let's make the most of them."

He eases me back onto the bed, runs his hands over me,

soft and gentle, then situates me so that I'm lying on top of him. "Can I stay the night?"

"Yeah, always."

He'll be gone when I wake in the middle of the night, but that's all right. I know he has other people counting on him besides me, so I'll take what I can when I can get it.

I undress for him, strip him out of the clothes he's wearing, start at his toes and kiss all the way up his body. I take him inside of me and try my best to commit every move he makes and every word he says to memory.

I wake to a note on my nightstand: *Lunch after class today?* And I smile when I roll back over and feel the sheet brush against my bare skin. I'm still naked from the night before and the sensation brings me back.

Yes, I should have been in the shower fifteen minutes ago, but I close my eyes and try to go back there again instead. My hand slips beneath the sheet, and I grip the flesh of my hip the way he would. One hand on my hip and the other touching one breast and then the other. He truly likes my curves, loves my body and loves the way I react to him. I imagine him whispering to me, telling me I'm *so fucking hot* the way he did last night. I slide down the bed a bit, arch my back and imagine as I'm rubbing myself that it's him touching me and then pushing inside. *Fuck me,* I beg him, and he doesn't disappoint.

I float back down to earth when I hear Frannie and Reese laughing in the living room. Reese calls out, "I guess Damien is giving her a ride to campus this morning." To which Frannie adds, "He's giving her the ride of her life!"

Guess I wasn't being so quiet about it after all.

# Chapter Fifteen

DAMIEN

When I see the number on my phone, my body goes cold. I let it ring, once then twice then three times.

"Everything all right?" Eli asks.

I nod and hold my palm up as I answer. I don't say much, nothing but a *Yes, sir* here and there, and the call is over within a minute.

"What's up?"

"I have to report tomorrow."

"That's three days early."

"I know that."

He gets up and goes to the kitchen. I can hear him opening the cabinet and taking down the shot glasses. I should tell him to stop—I sat him down and told him he needs to quit drinking just yesterday—but I need something to quell what's raging inside of me so desperately right now.

I knock the shot back just as Mr. Oliveri comes walking

into the living room. He looks between me and his son. "What's going on?"

Eli goes to the kitchen to grab another glass and then pours three shots. "Our boy has to report tomorrow morning at what, oh-six hundred?"

My voice sounds robotic when I answer, "Eight o'clock."

Mr. Oliveri's face falls. "Tomorrow morning?"

Maybe I nod, maybe I don't. Just know that I can't manage the effort it takes to speak in this state I'm currently in. I feel numb, I feel cheated, I feel fucked over.

And I feel trapped.

I want to hop on my bike and speed to Grace right now. I want to hold onto her for every moment that I have left. But one look at Eli as he pours himself another shot, and I know I can't go to her just yet.

I push the third shot he poured for me back across the table. "This isn't going to help."

Eli is annoyed, he wants me to join in and give him the excuse he needs to numb himself like he's done just about every day since we got back, but I won't do it. He goes to pick up my shot glass and drain it when his father grabs his wrist.

"This ends now, son. You hear me?"

Eli rests the glass back down on the table, then rests his head in his hands.

"I can't leave you like this, Eli. You need to promise me you're going to follow through on what we talked about." When he doesn't answer, I raise my voice. "This isn't fair to me. Shit, do you even care? You know I have to live with what I did to Cooper, so don't let me get on a plane thinking that someday I'll be carrying the weight of what you're thinking of doing, too. Please don't do this to me, brother."

Normally I wouldn't talk so openly in front of Eli's father, but I don't have time to be tactful right now. And I'd never bring up Cooper like that, but again, I'm not thinking one hundred percent clearly right now.

As a rule, I try not to think about Cooper. I just can't bring myself to wade chest deep through the awful details of that night again. I've never told Grace the whole story. I told myself that I didn't want to burden her with it, but maybe it's just that I don't want Grace to know. Don't want her to know that I missed all the signs Cooper gave, that I flat-out ignored him in that critical moment when he needed me most. I shake it off, tell myself again that I'm not responsible for what Cooper did even though I don't believe it.

Eli is looking at me in a way that feels like he can see right into my head. He wipes at his eyes and then stands up to bring the liquor back into the kitchen. I hear the contents swish down the drain and then hear the bottle clink against whatever else is in the recycle bin.

"There's a meeting at St. Anne's tomorrow at noon," Mr. Oliveri tells him. "I'll go with you."

He nods once, looks to me and then to his father. "Sounds like a plan."

* * *

I don my dress blues before Mr. Oliveri drops me off at her place a few hours later. I can show up to base in my service uniform, that's what's expected, but I go for formal instead. It's what you'd wear to a black-tie event, a parade or a formal ceremony. Weddings, funerals—that sort of thing. It's what I hope to wear when I marry Grace someday. Maybe that's why I put it on.

"It'll be all right, Damien. I don't want you to worry about Eli. You take care of yourself and we'll take care of him."

I nod, hoping for the best where my friend is concerned. I feel so messed up right now, so powerless. I look to the back where I stashed my duffle, then grab my hat off the seat.

"I'll see you at five-thirty?"

"We'll be here."

Grace looks surprised when she opens the door, and smiles as she takes me in from head to toe. I went all out, medals and ribbons and everything. I'm standing at attention and I don't return her smile. I try, but just can't do it.

"Hot damn," Reese calls out from the kitchen.

"You clean up nice, Sergeant," Frannie adds from her spot on the couch.

Grace's expression changes as the moment drags on, and the girls, no doubt sensing the vibe, share a look and then retreat to one of the back bedrooms.

"You're leaving."

"I just got the call. I'm due to report tomorrow morning." She looks around me to see if anyone else is outside. "Eli's father just dropped me off. They're coming back to get me at five-thirty. I just assumed that I'd—"

"Stay with me."

"Yes."

She stands up on her toes and places a soft kiss on my lips. "We'll make it a night to remember."

And it's not all doom and gloom, not the sad farewell I was dreading. No, Grace makes a point of ordering fried chicken that's a close second to the world-famous chicken we shared on our first date, in addition to mashed potatoes, macaroni dripping with cheese, and she even tacks on some steamed green beans and corn fritters so that I eat some vegetables. And after the girls clear out to catch a movie in town, I hear a knock on the door twenty minutes later to discover a bag with two pieces of banana cream cheesecake inside—my favorite.

Grace uncorks a bottle of wine and sets the table for us. She's keeping up a brave front, but I know she feels the same way I do. Taking a seat across from me, she raises her glass to mine. "Here's to the future, Sergeant Erikson."

"To the future," I repeat, clinking my glass against hers.

I notice she takes a big gulp of her wine before saying, "I hope your first leave is stateside and that it's soon."

I smile at her, knowing that's optimism and not reality. I doubt I'll be seeing Grace anytime before next summer at the very earliest, but I don't need to tell her that now.

"Be right back," I tell her as I go into her room. I have a pair of sweats I left here and a t-shirt , and I do change out of my dress blues into them, but first I tuck the letter I wrote to Grace in the top drawer of her nightstand.

I wrote it a few days ago, back in that basement cafeteria she took me to the first day we had lunch together. I sat down about an hour before I was scheduled to meet up with Grace, then proceeded to pour my heart out onto two pages, both back and front. I haven't read it over since that afternoon, for fear that I'll find it too sappy, too desperate, too something. I think I covered just about everything I'm feeling in that letter, and screw being embarrassed, it's best if she knows exactly where I stand.

"I can't show up with grease on my uniform, and the elastic waistband," I snap at my sweats, "means that I can stuff myself full of fried chicken."

"The girls were right. You do look like something out of a dream in your uniform."

"You like a man in uniform, huh?"

"I like *my* man in a uniform."

"I'll put it back on after we finish dinner if you want." That earns me a laugh. "We can role play."

"No thanks. I'll take you buck naked."

"Yes, ma'am."

We wrap the leftovers up after barely making a dent. We've been joking around and laughing, but the air is heavy with the goodbye that's bearing down on us. She plates one piece of cake and pours us each another glass of wine. With the two shots I did with Eli before, I'm starting to feel my alcohol, so I vow to go slow. What happens between us tonight is going to comfort me and hurt me—there's no way around it—but I want to remember every moment, the good and the sad.

She leads me into the bathroom in her room after we force ourselves to eat a few tasteless bites. Grace strips out of her clothes, turns the shower on and then steps into the steamy mist. I stand outside the shower watching as the water wets her hair and runs over her skin. She opens her eyes and reaches a hand out in invitation when she sees me still standing there, and as I tug the shirt over my head and push the sweats off my hips, I tell myself something I know all too well: *This is the last time.*

Having Grace in my life these past few weeks makes this all so much harder. I didn't know what I was missing before, but now I do. I know what her skin feels like, slick and wet in the shower pressed up against mine. I know how she sounds when I make her come. I know what it feels like to wake up and see that some beautiful girl has been watching you sleep, and I know how good her kisses feel.

I know Grace and I know that I want to spend the rest of my life with her.

As she comes down from it, her back still pressed against the tiles and her legs still wrapped around me, I raise up a silent prayer that I'll know this feeling again.

# Chapter Sixteen

## GRACE

He usually leaves without a word, slips out in the middle of the night without making a sound.

I sit up with a start, dragging in a breath as my eyes scan the room. He wouldn't leave without saying goodbye this time, would he?

My pounding heart calms when I see the bathroom light peeking out from underneath the door and I hear the faucet running. A minute later he comes back into the room, dressed except for his jacket and hat.

I turn my lamp on and wipe the sleep from my eyes. Looking him over, I take a moment to study the crisp pleats on his pants and shirt sleeves, the perfect shine on his shoes. I don't know this side of Damien. And while I admire the impressive form Sergeant Erikson makes in his uniform, I'm saddened by it even more.

"They'll be here in a few minutes."

"I know."

He takes a seat on the bed next to me. "I love you, Gracie girl."

"I love you too."

Damien rests his forehead against mine. There's nothing left to say.

A minute passes before the glare of headlights turning into the driveway signals the end.

"Don't walk me to the door," he says, whispering the words into my hair. "This is too hard as it is."

I nod, unable to speak past the lump in my throat.

He stands up, crosses the room and grabs his coat and hat off the chair. Damien doesn't look back when he says, "Write to me," before walking out and closing the door behind him.

* * *

I stay up and watch the sunrise. Watch as the sky turns from ink black to a cool pale gray. There is no sunshine, no clear blue sky, and I'm glad for it.

Listening to the saddest ballads on my playlist and keeping to my room to avoid my roommates' well-intentioned words of comfort, I spend the day reading and rereading the letter Damien tucked into my top drawer last night.

I can barely catch my breath at times, his words hitting me so deep in my soul that it feels like a physical blow.

Some parts of the letter give me hope for the future, but he's also prepared me for the worst case scenario. I know what he does is dangerous, but I've never really thought about the possibility of Damien not making it back. And it makes me so deeply sad to know that he's thinking about it, about the very real possibility of losing his life.

*Tis better to have loved and lost than never to have loved at all.*

Aunt Viv was the one who introduced me to Tennyson's so-called words of wisdom, and I was never a believer. Is it better? To me it's like Tennyson is saying that you're screwed either way.

With shaking hands, I put the letter away, tucking it between the pages of my journal.

I crawl into the bed that feels too big and so empty without him, and cry myself to sleep.

It won't be the last time.

# Part Two

## CHASING SHADOWS

# Chapter Seventeen

PRESENT DAY...

GRACE

"That doesn't bother you? You're way more understanding than I am."

"Hmm?" I look to my friend. "What did you say?"

Skylar lifts her chin, directing my attention to the other side of the room where my fiancé—I hate that word, by the way—is center stage surrounded by his students. "That grad assistant is practically drooling on your man's collar. I feel like going over there to offer her a napkin."

"Elizabeth?" I wave Skylar off. "She's harmless."

"Whatever you say, G."

That painful blast from the past gets my attention. "Do *not* call me G unless you want me to start calling you S."

"S sounds weird. Shortening a name only works with certain initials like G, E, B, T, D...Maybe even H. Nope, that sounds weird."

"I'm not a G."

She nods with a raised eyebrow. "Gotcha, Grace."

We're at some faculty banquet, one of many that I'm forced to attend on the arm of my boyfriend, Jack. That's right, boyfriend. I will no longer be using the F-word.

I look over to where he's standing, and maybe Skylar's right, his graduate teaching assistant is a little bit too close. I chuckle to myself when I see that she's now wearing glasses. Is she trying to emulate her academic idol, or her love interest, as Skylar suspects? She's laughing now, her head thrown back as if Jack has just said something hilarious. I imagine him telling her that joke about how many Marxists it takes to change a light bulb.

I should walk over there. The other students are involved in their own side conversations now, so maybe I should interrupt their little tête à tête, but I just can't muster up the energy.

And therein lies the problem.

Last night Jack looked frustrated after we, um, made love. That's his expression, not mine. I don't like the sound of it. *Making love.* The English language has been around for how many centuries now? Fourteen or fifteen? And in all that time we haven't come up with anything better than make love, have sex, do it, shag or fuck. And given those choices, I'll take fuck any day of the week. But Jack and I don't fuck. That word implies reckless abandon and it requires trust.

I remember the first time I heard that Nine Inch Nails song. I mean, they seriously got it. To fuck is to let go of your inhibitions, ignore all the mental chatter that weighs us down, and just go with our animal instincts. To lose yourself in touching, smelling and tasting—to feel.

Anyhoo, I digress. After makin' lurv, Jack looked frustrated and then accused me of being somewhere *far away*.

Has he just noticed this now? When I'm in bed with Jack all I do is think. I make the requisite sounds, I move my body—I'm not exactly a dead fish, but I'm not exactly present, either. I don't know how to be in the moment with him. Jack is a good man and he treats me like gold, but he's not Damien.

It's not even remotely fair to compare the two of them. Damien died when everything was new and golden between us. He'll always be forever young, and he is someone I've built up in my heart and in my mind for more than a decade.

I'm not a kid anymore, so I have to stop living in the past. I've been with Jack for nearly four years, and he's been steady and dependable, day in and day out. *Grow up, Grace.* I probably scold myself with those words at least once a week.

Chancing another look their way, I see that Elizabeth is now whispering in his ear. And is that a tumbler of whiskey in Jack's hand? He was drinking wine before.

I turn back to Skylar and Leo, deciding in that moment that if Jack wants to explore the dark side with Elizabeth tonight then he can have at it. Maybe that will finally give me the excuse I've been so desperately looking for, the one that will allow me to extricate my finger from this too-tight band and give it back to him. I've stared down at my ring finger every day for the past year since he proposed to me, and try as I might, I can't see a happily ever after for us.

"Hi, Grace."

I look up, a question in my eyes as I take in the man before me. "Um, hi."

Skylar nudges my elbow. "Spacey Gracie, I was just introducing you to our friend, Owen."

My face reddens. "Sorry about that, Owen. It's nice to meet you." I turn and shoot Skylar a look. "You're full of sass tonight. If you were still my student I'd send your butt to detention."

To that, Skylar sticks out her tongue and then smiles. "Too bad for you I'm a grown-up now."

"Your student?"

I laugh and take a sip of the refill Leo just placed in my hand. "Oops, I've dated myself. Yes, Skylar was my student."

"Grace was like the young, hot teacher at my high school." She tilts her head in an apology and smiles at me before looking back to their friend. "She was also, hands down, the best teacher I've ever had."

"Aw, shucks. I guess I have to forgive you for the Spacey Gracie thing now, don't I?"

Skylar pops another cheese cube into her mouth and nods as Leo says, "Owen teaches in the history department."

"Oh." I can't help but feel disappointed for some reason when I ask the obvious, "You're a professor at Pitt?"

"I just took a position here last year." His brow is furrowed. "What about you?"

I shake my head as if being a tenured college professor is a fate worse than death. "I still teach high school English. It'll be eleven years this coming September."

"Where?"

"About an hour south of here...Fayette County."

It feels like he's studying me for a few quiet moments before he says, "Eleven years is a long time and high school is a tough gig. I don't think I could handle all that drama."

"The staff causes more drama than the teenagers."

He looks around the room and then back to me. "Same here. A decade is a long time, though, so you must love your job."

*No.*

That's the first word that pops into my head.

I'm tired, and I'm not excited when I walk into the building every morning the way I used to be. I still love my students, but I'm sick of the school board looking to tie my hands at every turn and I'm tired of having to defend myself. But I paste on my smile when I answer, "I do, I love it."

"So what brings you here tonight?"

Leo and Skylar are talking to one of Leo's engineering buddies, so now it's just me and Owen. One quick glance in Jack's direction tells me he probably hasn't even noticed my absence. Yep, he's still in deep conversation with his gal Friday. *Hmm, I wonder if we share the same ring size?*

I look back to Owen and take him in, looking more closely now. He's got a strong build, like maybe he works out way too much and he's vain. His suit is well-tailored, and his sandy blonde hair is cut in a short but stylish way. Ugh, he probably pays more than I do for haircuts. He has a nice face, I'll give him that. Everything is in proportion. His mouth is the right size for his face, not too small the way Jack's is. *Sorry, Jack.* And his eyes, which I suddenly notice are an unusual, piercing shade of light blue, are at once icy and...amused.

"Grace?" He's chuckling when he says my name, the subtle laugh lines visible at the corners of his eyes and around his mouth.

"Yes?"

"Where'd you go? I was just asking what brings you here tonight."

"Sorry." I shake my head and absently look at the sparkly stone that feels like a boulder weighing me down. "I just have a lot on my mind."

His eyes follow the path mine have taken, and once he sees the ring his expression changes. "You're engaged?"

"I think so?"

That earns me another laugh. "And I thought tonight would be boring."

I try to return his smile but can't. "It was nice meeting you, Owen."

"You're heading out?" Skylar asks as she makes her way back over.

"I think so. Tell Leo I said goodnight and give Libs a hug for me, ok?"

She hugs me and whispers, "Will do."

When I look back to him, I see that his expression has taken a sympathetic turn. Maybe I'm easier to read than I thought. "Bye, Owen."

"Good luck, Grace."

* * *

"We need to talk."

I open the door and wave him inside.

Jack has been blowing up my phone since I left without telling him last night and drove home. I was supposed to stay at his place, but that pointed question left me emotionally wrecked. *You're engaged?*

*What am I doing?* That's what I repeatedly asked myself while speeding down Route 51.

Jack looks disheveled. He's always meticulous, so carefully put together, but right now his shirt is wrinkled, his eyes are bloodshot and his hair is sticking out in ten different directions. His shirt. It's the same one he wore last night.

"You just take off like that and then ignore my calls? I was looking all over for you, Grace! And can you imagine how embarrassed I was when I caught Leo Hale at the coat check and he told me you'd already left?"

Jack was embarrassed. Of course he was. The man hates to look bad, especially in front of his *colleagues*. That's another stuffy word he insists on using. Co-workers is a term better suited for manual laborers in his opinion, so I use it on purpose when I refer to my fellow teachers.

He held his tongue last night when he saw what I was wearing to the event because he knows better, but I could tell he was itching to say something. I've always liked clothes that are colorful, but sometimes I go overboard just to yank Jack's chain. Last night I went with a fire engine red wrap dress paired with my biggest gold hoop earrings, and while it's not like the other women were dressed for a funeral or anything, I know I stood out. Mission accomplished.

He's pacing the floor now, waiting on me to apologize, I think, but that's not happening. "I'm surprised you even noticed."

"What's that supposed to mean?"

"Have you been hooking up with Elizabeth?"

Jack has the nerve to look shocked by my question. "What?"

"I think you heard me."

"No! What would make you even think that? Jesus, Grace, we're engaged."

I look down at the ring. "She was all over you last night and it was obvious that you were enjoying the attention."

He takes a deep breath. "You were jealous?"

He's relieved, and in that moment I feel so sad and so guilty. Jack wants so much to believe that I care, that the mere sight of another woman beside him would make me storm out of that event in a fit of jealousy.

There's something I need to say but I'm struggling. I talk a good game, but deep down I'm afraid of being alone. Jack is not my soulmate—if such a thing even exists—but he's been my companion. Maybe I'm not over the moon when it comes to my feelings for Jack, but I do care about him. And as the words push up and past my lips, I know I'm about to set something into motion that can't be stopped.

"I don't know what it is that you see in me." No, I'm not looking for him to list my good qualities right now. "What I mean to say is, I don't think you really know me."

He's amused and hurt at once. "And whose fault is that?"

He walks over to my bookshelf and scans the top shelf until he finds that well-worn copy of *Hatchet*. Stupid on my part, to leave that small envelope in Damien's favorite book. Naturally Jack would have flipped through that one when he was bored and looking for something to read. It stands out among the love stories and poetry that I prefer.

That's the one and only book of boyhood adventure that I've read, and I've read it cover to cover so many times now that I can probably recite it word for word. For him. I read it to get into his head, to stay close to him, to have some piece of Damien.

He bends the spine of the short book and uses his thumb to run through the pages until he comes to where the envelope is tucked inside. I want to grab for it, protect it, keep it to myself.

"Who was this guy to you? I know you dated him back in college, but that's all you told me. Why do you still keep these pictures tucked away?" He studies the first one he takes out of the envelope, his expression pained as he shakes his head. "You look so happy."

He shows me so that I can see what he's talking about but I

don't need to look. I know every one of those photographs down to the most minute detail, and I know my face is lit up with the love I feel for Damien in every single one of them.

My first instinct is to say, *Be careful.* Those three pictures are all I have left of him, and they're far more precious to me than the two-carat diamond ring Jack put on my finger. I don't want so much as one of Jack's fingerprints on the surface, let alone for him to bend or otherwise damage it in a flash of anger. With the care of a hostage negotiator, I hold out my palm and he places the picture in it. I hold out my other palm for the envelope and I'm thankful when he hands that over too.

"His name is Damien."

"I know his name, it's written on the back. But why do you still keep his picture? Are you still in love with the guy?"

I shake my head. How can I even answer that question? To say the words out loud, that yes, I am in love with a dead man, is to admit to Jack that I've been dishonest from day one.

But I will not dishonor Damien. I can't.

"He died, Jack...A long time ago." I don't even realize that I'm holding the pictures against my heart until I see his eyes fixed there. "There's a part of me that will always love him."

"You're the only person I've ever loved, Grace, so maybe I just don't know any better. I take what you give me and I'm happy for it. But you never look at me the way you're looking at him in those pictures." He takes his glasses off and pinches the bridge of his nose. "I don't think you're in love with me. I don't think you ever were."

"It's not you—"

He stops me. "It's not you, it's me. Are you seriously about to feed me that line of crap?"

But in this case it's the truth. He's done nothing wrong. The way I am, this closed-off version of myself who's been sleepwalking through the past fifteen years of my life? All this time, he didn't stand a chance.

I can tell him now and try to make him understand. I can tell him about Damien, about the pregnancy, about our daughter, about the warm and precious bundle I held only once. I can tell Jack how empty my arms have felt since the social worker took her from me. I can tell him about the despair I felt in the days and months that followed. And how the black cloud of that combined loss, of Damien and our baby, has followed me ever since.

"I can't believe this shit."

I almost smile at his choice of words because Jack doesn't curse. I wish he would. I wish he would have cursed and called me out on my bullshit years ago. I could have saved him from wasting his time on me.

"I'm sorry."

"You're sorry? All this time I've been competing with a ghost. This is so fucking ridiculous. You see that, don't you?"

When he sees me twisting the ring off my finger, he stops. "What are you doing, Grace?"

"Last night I must have looked over at you ten times. You were laughing, Jack. You looked happy with Elizabeth, like you were having a great time." He's about to protest so I gesture for him to stop. "I mean it...I never knew what it was that you saw in me."

He shakes his head. "You're kind, you're beautiful and you're caring. I love being with you."

"But you don't know me. There's so much about my past that you don't know. And before you say it, I know that's one hundred percent on me. I'm to blame."

Jack steps closer. "There's nothing you could tell me about your past that will change the way I feel. He's gone. I'm here and I'm telling you that I love you." He reaches out to put one gentle hand on my cheek. "I was angry last night. I let things build up instead of talking it out with you. And maybe I am guilty of playing games, of flirting and getting off on that kind of attention. But you know she means nothing to me. There's no one but you."

I put my hand over his, feeling more sure and steady than I have in a long time. He's searching my eyes and then his hand drops when he doesn't get the reassurance from me that he's looking for.

"Wait." I stop him as he turns to go. "Take this," I tell him as I place the ring in his palm and then close his fingers around it. "You're a good person, Jack, and you deserve so much more than what I can give you."

# Chapter Eighteen

## GRACE

"I told him." Kicking at the twigs and dead leaves in front of me, I decide to come absolutely clean. "I told him the basics, anyway. I didn't tell him about her."

I've only shared my secret with one other person in all these years. It's beyond bizarre when I think about it. My mother and father don't know, I never told my Aunt Viv, never told the men I've dated over the years or the one man who put a ring on my finger.

I let it slip just once, in one of those desperate moments when I saw my own fear mirrored in the eyes of one of my students. Charlotte Mason. I wonder where she is now. I wonder what decision she made back then.

It was just a hunch on my part. I mean, I would have bet the farm that she was pregnant when she showed up at my classroom that day, but I don't have any solid proof to back that theory up. She started cutting class, her grades took a nose-dive, she dropped her friends and she quit the dance club. The girl who was so conscientious and eager was morphing into a distracted mess right in front of my eyes. Having undergone that same transformation myself, I knew the signs all too well.

I never saw her again. She was gone, sent to live with family up in northern Michigan from what Mr. Vargas told me. She was a sweet kid and a great dancer, one of the best to walk into my tryouts. I don't think I did right by her. I didn't do enough. Northern Michigan—I shiver at the thought of it.

"It's too damn cold here," I tell him. "This is nothing like our spot."

This river flows the same as the Eno, but even in the winter months that followed after Damien left, when I went out there just to think and to remember, it never seemed as icy and bleak and this place. It's late spring, but I still can't imagine a crappie or any other fish surviving in this frigid water. *Crappies*. Saying it still brings a smile to my face.

"Maybe I should move to a warmer climate. Frannie is still in North Carolina and she has a beach house out in Nags Head. Did I tell you I went there last summer to meet up with the girls? It was the first time I'd seen them in nearly a decade."

He got along with Frannie and Reese, and they liked him too. I can still picture him blushing when Reese would let out with some lewd joke. She was, and still is, a badass. I bet we all would have stayed close if things had turned out differently. It's kind of amazing to me that we're still in touch at all. I pretty much morphed into a zombie junior year. I made a slow recovery senior year but was nowhere back to my old self.

The girls knew Damien died overseas. Frannie actually found out before I did. But they didn't know the rest. They didn't know I spent the following summer in our off-campus apartment alone, riding out the last trimester of my pregnancy. I never told them that I was scared out of my mind when my water broke, or that I called a cab to take me to the hospital. They don't know that I gave birth to a beautiful baby girl, or that I handed her over to two strangers the next day.

I lied to them every time they asked me if I wanted to talk in those days and weeks right after Damien shipped out, lied to them every morning when I was sick, and then lied when I wore loose shirts and flowy sundresses towards the end of the spring semester. They knew something was very wrong, but they chalked it up to the loss of Damien.

I heard Reese comment to Frannie once, something about the two of us only being together for a few weeks and how my reaction was, in her opinion, *beyond*. But I couldn't even get angry because she didn't know the half of what I'd lost.

What I gave away.

"Reese has four kids now, can you believe it? I always pictured Frannie as the mother figure...Reese, not so much. Four boys and they look like hell raisers." I smile my same heavy smile when I think of Damien. "You would have been a great father."

There's no doubt in my mind, and it hits like an arrow to the heart whenever I let my mind go there.

I picture our little girl at around age four of five, like Skylar and Leo's Olivia. Ink black hair that's grown halfway down her back, following her dad around and asking *Why?* every time Damien pauses to do some part of his elaborate campsite set-up routine.

He'd explain every step with patience, and with an intensity that tells her survival skills are something his little girl should learn, no different from a little boy. I picture her standing beside him on the bank of the river as Damien teaches her to cast off the way he taught me. I picture her sitting on his lap near the campfire as I tackle the one task where my skills exceed her father's: making s'mores. And then I picture myself leaning over, my daughter laughing as I kiss a wayward bit of melted chocolate as it lands on her cheek.

I've pictured her at every age, on every single one of her birthdays and on the days in between. I've spent countless hours daydreaming of holding her in my arms as an infant. That tuft of black hair on her little head, her rosy puckered lips, the eyes so much like her father's that I wept whenever she opened them that day.

What is she like now? It's a question I ask myself so often.

She turned fourteen last August. I try not to think of myself at that age, but it's hard. I was a hot mess at fourteen. Reeling from my parents' divorce, I doubted everything I did, said, wore, and even thought. Older and wiser, with years to observe that same kind of emotional turmoil in the students I serve, now I can cut myself a break, tell myself I did the best I could whenever I get stuck in the bad memories.

*You're too hard on yourself, Grace.*

"And you're too easy on me, Damien."

He always built me up, reworked my past so I'd think of myself as a resilient person who came through a tough time on top. A fighter. I wonder sometimes, does he hate me for not fighting when it came to her?

To ease the ache in my heart, I picture her smiling, surrounded by friends and making her way through high school with her head held high.

God, I hope she's faring better than I did. I hope she's confident, outspoken, and stands up for herself. I pray she's been well cared for. The couple I met through pictures and a bio that was written like a sales pitch, I pray every single day that they're good to her.

# Chapter Nineteen

GRACE

"We're having a party next Saturday and you have to come. Jack too, of course."

I haven't told anyone about the break-up. It's only been a few days so I'm not about to go beating myself up over my lack of transparency. This lie of omission is nothing like the others.

"What's the occasion?" I ask Skylar.

"Well, I just finished my first year as a gainfully employed, bona fide kindergarten teacher and I survived. I'd say that's reason enough to celebrate."

"It definitely is. I'm thinking you more than just survived it, though."

"I did totally love it, but dealing with twenty kindergarteners day after day can wipe you out. I'm ready for a break."

"I think I could handle the kiddos, it's those snobby Fox Chapel parents who would have me hopping the first bus bound for Betty Ford."

"They weren't so bad. The parents are way more obnoxious at private schools like Olivia's."

In the background I hear Olivia ask what obnoxious means, and laugh to myself as Skylar gives the most complimentary definition she can think of.

"Determined? You mean, determined to drive their precious offspring's teacher into an early grave?"

"Something like that," she whispers on a giggle. "So, can you come on Saturday?"

"Who's going to be there?"

"We invited a few of Leo's work buddies, two girls that I work with and their husbands, and Sienna and Garth will be here, too." Before I can answer, she says, "And why do I have to sell this to you, Grace? Talk about obnoxious."

She's right, so I apologize and then tell her I'd love to come. "What can I make?"

"Some of those lemon bars you used to bring to school would be awesome."

"I can't believe you remember that."

"I love food, what can I tell you? You used to bring them to our creative writing club meetings and you baked for the dance team, too."

"I wish I didn't love baking as much as I do. I wind up sampling the goods way more often than I should."

"You look fantastic! And you just reminded me, Leo opened the pool last week so bring a suit."

I'm thinking out loud when I say, "Great," with no enthusiasm.

Skylar, who has the benefit of being a full decade younger than me, has the nerve to laugh. "Don't worry, stacked is in style."

As I end the call, I walk into my tidy little kitchen and pour myself a glass of wine. Classes finished a few days ago, and just last night I stood on stage to help hand out the diplomas. It's always an emotional evening and it always brings up memories. I imagine it's the same for all of us teachers and the administrators.

Grabbing a bag of popcorn from the counter, I take my glass and settle onto the couch. But instead of turning on the television or grabbing my tablet to read, I just sit there thinking about graduation.

Hair curled or gelled to perfection, make-up applied with care and neckties worn for the first time, their smiles were infectious last night. The excitement of it all, the promise of good things to come—I felt it, too.

Some of them are going on to community college, some to impressive universities, and some will be entering the work-force. Whatever path they've chosen, graduation is a time of change and transition, and it's a big deal.

I signed my contract for next year with a heavy heart. I'm due for a change too, but I chose to stay rooted in place. I tell myself that I can't leave, that I have too many loose ends to tie up, but it's a lie. I used to say that I couldn't leave Aunt Viv, and while that was true, she did need me to manage her affairs, the woman I knew and loved no longer recognized me. I managed her caregiver's schedules, dealt with her doctor, picked up her prescriptions and made sure that her grocery order was delivered twice a week, but I used the responsibility as an excuse. I could have left years ago. And now she's gone, so why am I still here?

The spring semester was brutal. It's not the kids. I can handle the disruptive students, the emotionally needy students, and I can handle mediating fights, addressing mean girl behavior and consoling my kids when they lose games, opportunities, parents or their first loves.

My discontent comes from within. It's like Groundhog Day when my alarm goes off in the morning. My life is starting to feel like trudging waist-deep through mud, and I'm finding it harder and harder to hold myself together without screaming.

I want to scream.

I want to broadcast my secrets in the town square or from the pulpit at Sunday Mass. I want to come clean and then live free of this burden that I've carried for more than a decade.

# Chapter Twenty

OWEN

"How does it feel?"

"It fucking hurts." I wince but then force a smile when I see dismay on the face of Ben's graduate assistant. "Same way it always does the first week or two. It's good, I'll get used to it."

Ben is crouched down by where my left knee used to be, all but snickering. "You'll get used to it."

"What are you, a damn parrot?"

Being that he's more than familiar with my grumpy ass, he ignores me and goes about adjusting my shiny new toy. "You're going to love how this baby reacts on stairs."

His graduate assistant covers her mouth to hide her smile when she says, "You sound like a car salesman, Professor Tillman."

Ben turns to her and taps on my new leg. "Zero to six miles an hour in under ten seconds flat. And did I mention it's waterproof?"

"I can go in the water with this?" I'm legit shocked. "I won't damage the microprocessor?"

"Nope. The X3 is made for complete submersion. Some people prefer to swim without it, though, so whatever floats your boat."

I think back to last summer, feeling a sense of accomplishment after finishing my workout, only to find that the lifeguard had moved my gear bag from the side of the pool without asking. Had to hop over to retrieve it, garnering the attention of more than a few people in the process. And whenever that happens I get one of three reactions. You get the people who fix their eyes on my leg for a nanosecond and then look away, embarrassed to be caught staring. Then you have the ones who make eye contact and smile, as if they're granting me acceptance or pity or what the fuck ever. My least favorite are the ones who want to engage me in conversation, who want to forge some bond for reasons unknown.

Some thank me for my service without even knowing my story. I did indeed get injured serving my country, but nowadays it's like an assumption. I always want to shake my head, point to my leg and say something like: *rodeo accident*.

I love being in the water—there's nothing like it—but transitioning in and out of a pool, the ocean, or any body of water can be awkward, and something I prefer to do when I'm alone or among friends.

"Run me through this again. I was invited to a pool party tomorrow, so maybe I'll take this baby for a dip."

They walk me through attaching and removing the device three more times. When we're finally done, the both of them stand side by side like two proud parents as I take the stairs with ease on my way out. Leaning over the railing, Ben calls out, "Text me, all right? I want to know how the swimming goes."

When Leo invited me to their summer kick-off party last week, I can't say I was excited. And it wasn't the mention of a pool party that had me feeling ambivalent. Nope, it's just that I know how this shit goes. Single girls, single guys, a couple here and there. The expectation that you'll connect with someone is heavy on the minds of the well-meaning hosts and it weighs on me, too.

I'm thirty-five, fresh off a break-up, and I'd be lying if I said it feels like nothing is missing from my life. I have a job that I love, a supportive family and I have friends. I'm not lonely, but in every way that's important, I am alone.

My need for companionship, for love, for sex—I almost stayed with Ava because of it. But after six months you either feel it or you don't, and I wasn't feeling forever.

Another chink in my chain is the probability of having to endure this party alongside Skylar's friend, Grace, and her fiancé. Sky pointed him out to me after Grace ran out of that faculty dinner like Cinderella, and I wanted to slap the shit out of the guy without even knowing the first thing about him. The only thing that gave me pleasure was watching him scan the room for a good fifteen minutes after she left. The fucker looked nervous and it served him right. When you have a woman like Grace, you don't pull what he did.

Listen to me, *a woman like Grace*. I don't know the first thing about her. I mean, she's hot—doesn't take much to ascertain the obvious—and she seems like she has a good sense of humor. From the few exchanges I overheard between her and Skylar, I would even say she's a bit of a smart ass. She's came off like a bit of a dingbat too, but maybe I just caught her on an off night.

Something about her drew me in like a bear to honey. Again, she's hot, so no surprise there, but it was more than that. What exactly? The only thing I can come up with is that she made me smile.

That sexy red dress tied at the waist with a scarf that looked like part of a belly-dancer's outfit, complete with shiny metal discs sewn into the fabric. Dark red lipstick that made her full lips beg, in my warped mind, for a hungry kiss. And the way she absently swayed in time to the background music, as if she couldn't help but move in a way that called out to me. In that moment I wanted to take her by the hand, walk her outside and dance with her under the night sky. No words, no negotiation, nothing but her body moving with mine.

Reality hit like a bucket of cold water when I followed her eyes down to that ring on her finger.

Grace belongs to someone else.

Skylar stood up for her man when I made a comment about Grace kicking his ass to the curb. Skylar said he was solid and then waved me off, telling me I didn't know the whole story when I disagreed with her glowing praise of the guy.

I saw nothing but doubt in Grace's eyes when she looked down at her finger, and in that moment I felt like the two of us were kindred spirits or some shit. I wanted to tell her to rip the bandage off, to take the hard road instead of going through with something that in her heart she knew was wrong. I was in that same place just a few months ago. I hurt Ava badly—she still calls to let me know just that—but I know I did the right thing.

And I'll do the right thing this weekend. I'll be open-minded, I'll meet some new people, and I'll stay the hell away from Grace.

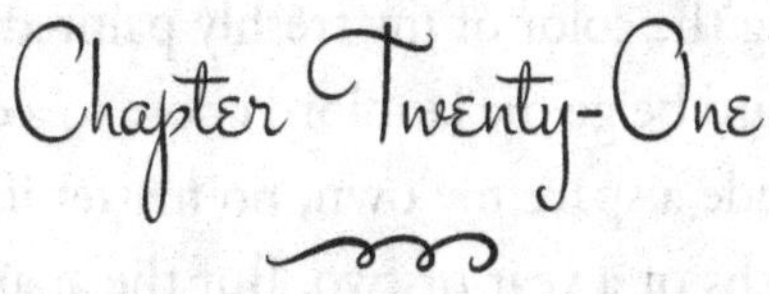

# Chapter Twenty-One

## GRACE

Studying myself in the mirror, I make another slow rotation and have to concede that I don't look half bad. It's my thirty-fourth birthday today, and while a few pesky lines have made an appearance here and there, my skin still looks good, dancing and yoga have kept my muscles toned, and my hair is behaving for my special day.

I made a trip up to Pittsburgh on Wednesday, as this one-horse town doesn't have squat in terms of remotely fashionable clothing stores, and spent an entire afternoon trying on more bathing suits than I could count. I don't know if it's the birthday thing or what, but I was feeling particularly ballsy when I picked out this one-piece number that has so many cutouts that it might as well be a string bikini. It's dark plum, which is a departure from my usual kaleidoscope of a color palette, and it compliments the tan I achieved by laying out in Viv's backyard a few times this week.

I still call it Viv's backyard, Aunt Viv's house. I can't help it. I used to be a nester. Freshman year of college I decorated my tiny corner of our dorm room with string lights, posters, potted plants and all of the knickknacks I collected over my short lifetime. When we moved off-campus I stepped it up a notch, changing the color of my freshly painted bedroom walls from the standard beige the landlord chose to a cheery yellow.

I always made a space my own, no matter if I was staying a couple of months or a year or two. But the apartment I rented when I first graduated never got that treatment. It never felt lived in or inviting. I just didn't have it in me to admit that this might be permanent. And since I inherited Aunt Viv's house, it's basically remained a shrine to the years she spent here.

Aside from the one project I've completed: stripping the garage down to its bare bones to make it into a no-frills studio, I've left it alone. I tend to the garden and clean like a banshee, but I haven't changed the outdated wallpaper or so much as a light fixture. My things are here but this place isn't home. I can't settle in, can't settle for this life.

Inspecting myself up close, I'm pleased by the smooth skin of my bikini line, and I'm glad I also splurged for a manicure and a pedicure at that swanky South Hills day spa. I tell myself I've done this for me and me alone, and while it's true that I've learned the value of self care over the years, maybe the reality of being single again has me upping my game.

I make the drive up, wondering who's going to be there, and while I'm not actively looking for anyone or anything, I'm just hoping I won't be the one lone ranger in a sea of happy couples. I've been in that position before and it's not even remotely fun.

Pulling into the driveway, I see my happy hostess clipping some bright pink hydrangeas with the little girl who is hers in every way except through birth. Turning at the sound of my car, she tosses the blooms to the grass and takes Olivia by the hand. "Look who's here, Libs!"

"Hi, ladies. I like the matching get-ups."

Skylar looks down to Olivia and says, "Libs is a trend setter, aren't you?"

Olivia comes over and wraps her arms around my waist like an octopus. For some reason she's fascinated with me, even though I've taken pains to keep my distance.

The first time she plopped herself into my lap I lost track of what I was saying, and then found myself nuzzling her curly blond hair to get my fill of that yummy strawberry-scented shampoo. It hit me like a drug, and I was no sooner falling down the rabbit hole. *Birdie*, I heard myself whispering into her hair, imagining for a moment that she was mine—that she was my girl.

I rustle Olivia's hair and twist my body to break her hold in a way that I hope isn't obvious. This has been a week, as Aunt Viv used to say, and while I've managed to keep it together, I can do without this little girl loving on me right now.

"I like your pretty dress," she says, looking up at me as if I'm some wonderful, exotic creature.

Olivia is good for my confidence, I'll give her that.

"Thank you, sweetie." I take a step back to admire her dress. "Your dress is divine." Heavy on the drama, I tell her that purple is one of my absolute favorite colors.

She gestures for me to lean down, and when I do she cups her hand over my ear and whispers, "Is today really your birthday?"

Ugh. I straighten up and roll my eyes at a very guilty-looking Skylar.

"Jack mentioned it."

"Please tell me you're not going to make this a thing."

"I wrapped your present all by myself!"

Olivia's enthusiasm makes me feel like a party pooper, so I suck it up and smile because I'm being an idiot. Birthdays are meant to be fun, to be celebrated. And while I will strangle Skylar if she tries to make me the center of this party, I can't go on pouting in front of a five-year-old about having to blow out candles on a cake while people sing to me. Talk about first-world problems.

I crouch down to her level. "You are so sweet to think of me on my birthday. And I can't wait to open my present."

Turning to Skylar, she asks, "Can we give it to her right now?"

"It's up to Grace."

"Lead the way," I tell Olivia, who still has my hand gripped in hers.

"The guest of honor has arrived!" Leo greets me as we walk into the kitchen.

From the corner of my eye I can see Skylar giving him the cut throat gesture before she says, "Ix-nay on the irthday-bay."

Olivia ignores them both and rushes over to where a box wrapped in bright pink paper sits on the coffee table. There's a giant white bow on the top and my name is written in purple letters surrounded by hearts.

"How beautiful!" And now I'm gushing for real, because it's obvious from the wrinkled paper, the clumps of tape and the immature handwriting that Olivia has, in fact, done this all by herself, and the effort she's put into making my day special has me choking up.

When I open the box and lift my gift out from the mounds of tissue paper, I have to swallow the emotion down once again because I immediately recognize this blast from my past.

"Is this what I think it is?" I whisper as I slowly lift the top of the wooden case.

"Open it, open it," Olivia urges me on, so excited that she's bouncing on her feet and clutching her hands in front of her chest to contain her excitement.

As the twinkling first notes of Tchaikovsky's *Dance of the Sugar Plum Fairy* sound and the tiny ballerina begins to spin once she's free, I'm transported back to my childhood, daydreaming as I stood in front of my dresser, mesmerized by the delicate figurine and the music I knew by heart.

I wipe at a stray tear before I look back to Olivia smiling. "This is the best birthday present I've ever gotten. Thank you."

"It's *The Nutcracker*. Daddy is taking me and Sky to see it next Christmas."

"How fun! It's one of my absolute favorite ballets."

"Can you teach me?" she asks as she spins in breathless circles.

Under her breath, Skylar says to Leo, "Here we go," before laughing and pointing to me. "She's been itching for a trip down to see you. Olivia wants me, her and Sienna to take a dance lesson in your studio."

"Calling that beat-up garage a studio is a stretch but," turning back to Olivia, I say, "we can definitely run through the basics one day soon. Sure."

And for that I get another hug and multiple kisses on both cheeks. She's a trip.

Olivia busies herself opening and closing the top of the jewelry box as I head back into the kitchen.

Skylar takes a big bowl of potato salad out of the refrigerator and turns to me as she hip checks the door to close it. "Don't get mad at Jack. I think the birthday thing just slipped the other night."

Leo asks, "Where is he, anyway?"

"Couldn't make it. He had, um, a family thing."

Skylar looks like she wants to ask a follow-up question but thinks better of it. "Help me with this stuff, will you?" she asks as she hands me a tray of yummy looking sandwiches on mini croissants.

"These look so good."

"Half of them are gruyere, black forest ham, arugula and honey mustard, and the other half are roast beef and sharp cheddar with horseradish sauce. Oh, and Sienna made a tray of those crab cakes you love."

"You Perillo girls never disappoint in the food department."

"Excuse me," a snarky voice calls from behind us. "The Perillo girls don't disappoint in *any* department."

"Sienna!"

I put the platter down and grab my girl in a hug. Over the past year I've grown close with Skylar, and when you're close with Skylar, you're in with Sienna too. That's just how it is. It's funny, given that the two of them were my students five years ago, but both of them have lived through more in the past couple of years than many do in a lifetime. Maturity-wise, I feel like we're on even ground.

"How are you?"

"*So* good! She looks down at her stomach, drawing my attention to the bump, and then back up to me. "Did Sky tell you we're due in October?"

Skylar smiles and raises her eyebrows as she goes over to take her nephew from his father. "Hello, Garth...And no, I didn't tell anyone, Sienna."

Two babies only a year, no, eighteen months apart. I know Skylar worries about them, and I get it. But the two of them seem over the moon about life in general every time I see them, and their joy is infectious. I envy them. At their age I thought every single thing through, weighed the pros and cons and analyzed every potential outcome. Maybe I should have been more like the two of them: carefree and sure in the knowledge that everything will just work out.

Take a leap of faith? Back then I never would have dreamed of it. But then I smile thinking of that fist date with Damien. I was carefree with my arms wrapped tight around him and my hair whipping in the breeze on the back of his motorcycle. Allowing myself to fall in love with him when I knew there was so little time? That was a leap of faith. But I wish I'd had more faith in myself when it really mattered.

I give her a hug and then Garth. "Congratulations! I bet James can't wait to meet his new little brother or sister."

"Thanks, Miss Daw—I mean, thank you, Grace."

"He's still having a hard time with the transition." Sienna says as she rubs Garth's shoulder. "You'll always be Miss Dawson, English teacher extraordinaire in Garth's eyes."

"Not gonna lie...It is kinda weird to call you by your first name."

"Garth? I'm one year older as of eight o'clock this morning, so if you call me Miss Dawson today, you die."

# Chapter Twenty-Two

OWEN

I. Am. Dead.

I'm frozen in place, the beer bottle perched against my open lips as I catch sight of Grace stripping out of her sundress and then lowering herself into the pool.

A few of us are in the kitchen but most people are out in the backyard. The music changed from pop to country a few minutes ago, and Leo's buddy Max, who's playing DJ, was eating it up when a few of the girls broke into a sexy line dance. Grace was sandwiched between Skylar and a girl who has to be her twin, and the three of them were turning heads. When the song ended, the girls laughed when everyone started clapping and whistling, and that's when Grace lifted her hair up and wiped the sweat from her neck with her free hand.

She's hot, in both the literal and figurative sense of the word, and now it's like I'm watching the scene unfold in slow motion as she unties the sash at her waist and then opens herself up like a present to reveal the most rocking body I've seen in a long time. The girl has curves for miles, and her suit is made of crisscrossing strips of fabric that are struggling to rein them in.

I'm damn near drooling when Leo taps my shoulder and laughs, bringing me back down to earth. "Down, boy."

"Huh?"

"See something you like?"

I take a long pull off my beer, thankful that I'm off to the side and therefore out of sight for the most part. "Shut it, Leo. She's engaged last I heard."

He nods in agreement. "Last I heard." He shrugs, finishes his beer and takes my empty bottle before heading back towards the fridge. "Ben told me you're breaking out a new model today. What are you waiting for? Go get in the pool."

"Were all of you engineering nerds gossiping again?"

"We prefer to call it shop talk."

"It *is* pretty cool. I used my running attachment this morning, then swapped it back out and went on a ten-mile ride."

"Are you training for a triathlon?"

"Maybe." But my smile gives me away. "I'll start off with a sprint length and then hopefully work my way up."

"How is the carbon running foot?"

"Unbelievable, and the knee joint makes me stable on uneven surfaces when I'm running. It's everything, though. Basic activities like going up and down stairs are so much easier. I keep looking down at it, amazed."

"You can thank the engineering nerds for that."

"I do owe you nerds a debt of gratitude."

"So, are you going in?"

"I think I might wait until Monday. I'm meeting Ben at the pool on campus. I had to call him twice today to walk me through a few technical issues, just with interchanging the components. Easy stuff, but it's new to me."

"I like the shiny finish on this one," Skylar says as she opens and closes the screen door. "Way better than the skin tone. It's got that *Terminator* vibe."

"That's what I was going for."

"What are you all doing inside? There's burgers that need a grillin' and women who need dance partners."

And the way Leo answers, "At your service, baby," leaves me feeling more than just a little bit jealous. The looks and the words that pass between the two of them are something that I envy. I want what they have.

I walk around them with a sudden urge to escape, but my timing sucks.

As I step out into the yard, Grace is making her way back out of the pool, her hips swaying with each movement as she makes her way up the stairs. She reaches behind her when she's back on the deck, water dripping down her body as she tugs the fabric of her suit down to cover that gorgeous round ass. I have to look away. I'm damn near salivating for this woman I barely know, and there's a force drawing me towards her that's as powerful as it is senseless.

She belongs to another man.

I head towards a few guys over by the grill but don't make it halfway there before I'm intercepted.

"Hey, I know you."

Grace wraps herself in a towel, fastening the end before reaching up to free her hair from the band holding it in. I'm struck dumb for a moment as the curls tumble down and over her shoulders.

"Owen, right?"

"Yeah...Owen. It's nice to see you again, Grace. How are you?"

"I'm starving right now." She takes a whiff of what's cooking. "I might just kill to get one of the first cheeseburgers off the grill."

I can't help but laugh because she looks as if she just might resort to violence, and I like a girl who likes cheeseburgers.

I gesture over to a table. "Get us some beers and I'll take care of the chow."

"Sounds like a plan. Pickles, red onion and extra cheese on that bad boy, ok?"

"You got it. I'll be right back."

I'm doing an internal version of shaking my head as I pile her burger high with fixings and then load both of our plates with sides. I'm a glutton for punishment. Her man is probably late to the party, that's all, and now I'm going to get even closer to what I want just before the rug gets pulled out from underneath me. I decide that I'd rather get burned, though. Walking away right now just isn't an option.

And when I get to the table, I'm rewarded by the sight of Grace settled into a chair with the towel now discarded and pooled around her hips. And that suit? Minimal coverage. I get glimpses of her hips, her belly and her tits. She is like a goddamn work of art. After making a mental note to stop gawking, I set our plates down and take the beer from her outstretched hand. Grace is smiling up at me, and I must be stupid or something because I'm thinking to myself that she's got the best smile I've ever seen.

"This looks fantastic," Grace says as she lifts the bun and squirts some ketchup on the burger.

I am seriously pathetic, watching as she opens her mouth wide and takes a bite, closing her eyes and damn near moaning as her head rolls back. I can't look away. No, my eyes are glued to her the entire time like this show she's putting on is some grade-A porn.

Her eyes flutter open and she smiles when she says, "I haven't eaten all day. I had some coffee and that's it."

"I wake up starving." I pause to take a bite and then nod because it is delicious. "I would have passed out by now if I were you. This is my third meal of the day."

She looks amused when she says, "You wear it well. And just for the record, I usually do eat breakfast, but I was running around getting errands done this morning. And *maybe* I skipped because I ate more than just a few of the lemon bars I was baking last night for this party."

"Lemon bars, huh? I'll have to sample your goods later."

"You do that, Owen."

It's flirty the way she says it, and when she lifts the burger up to her mouth for another bite, I notice she's not wearing that rock on her left hand. I'm sure there's a reasonable explanation. More reasonable than the crazy hopes I'm floating right now. I'm hoping that dog is long gone and forgotten. I'm hoping Grace is single and not nursing a broken heart. And if she's even half as into me as I am into her, then I'm hoping—no—praying that I have a shot.

"So what's your story, Grace?"

"My story?" When I nod, she takes a forkful of potato salad and looks off into the distance as she chews. A moment later she says, "Well, I just signed on to teach for another year even though I want to quit my job, I just broke off my engagement, and oh, today is my birthday. And I'm on my third drink, so I'm a little tipsy. That," she tips her bottle to mine, "is my story."

I want to fist pump the universe for answering my prayer,

but I'm careful to school my expression. "Three drinks and you spill all your secrets? Good to know."

"Oh no," she shakes her head, "it would take a lot more than three drinks for me to spill the good stuff."

"Want a soda or some water?"

"I'd love some water. Thanks." And when I come back outside balancing two cups and two lemon bars, I see that Grace has cleaned her plate. "Do you want me to grab you another burger? There's some chicken over there, too."

"No, I'm stuffed. Oh, you found the lemon bars! You can have both of those, big guy." She pats her flat belly. "I don't think I have any room left."

"Seriously? I was just about to stick a candle in one of them and sing *Happy Birthday*."

"I'd kill you."

"Don't like birthdays?"

She shakes her head. "It's not that." She looks over her shoulder to where Skylar and a few of the other women are setting up lunch for the kids. "Skylar and Sienna are like party planning ninjas. I've already opened my present and I'm sure I'm going to be ambushed later on with a cake, fireworks and God knows what else."

"Sienna...They're twins, right?" I shake my head. "Don't even answer that dumb question. They look so much alike it's freaky."

Grace smiles. "They were a force to be reckoned with in high school."

"That's awesome. I haven't been at it long enough to be friends with any of my former students, but I imagine it would be nice."

"They're the only former students I'd consider friends. I teach in a small town, so I see my kids everywhere, but those two are the only ones with permission to call me by my first name."

I take a bite of the sweet cake. "Man, these are good."

"My Aunt Vivian's recipe. I've been making them since I was a teenager."

"Tell her I'm a fan."

Her smile is soft. "She passed away. Viv was a very special lady."

"I'm sorry."

"Thank you. Viv was eighty-one and she was not herself towards the end. Maybe in some ways it was a blessing. She was such a smart woman, so losing her cognitive skills probably felt like a slow form of torture."

"Dementia?" She nods as I shake my head. "That's the worst."

"Agreed." She watches me for a moment while I eat and then says, "Hey, thanks for not going all investigative reporter on me a few minutes ago when I aired my dirty laundry."

"The truth isn't dirty laundry. You just have stuff weighing on your mind."

"No one else knows about Jack."

"Your boyfriend?"

She nods. "Ex. And it was just a few days ago, so..."

"I get it. It's still in that messy stage." I answer the question in her eyes, "There's still the occasional phone call, you have to return the last of his things, or move out and settle the financial stuff if you were living together."

"We weren't living together." She looks up to the sky and shakes her head when she adds, "That would have been so much harder."

"I've been there, and it makes it one hundred percent harder to cut ties."

"You're assuming I was the one who did the breaking up, not him?"

I cover my smile by taking another sip of my beer. "You just told me you broke it off a few minutes ago." She palms her forehead. "And I would have assumed that's how it went down anyway. You didn't come off as content the night I met you."

"I think I came off like a scatterbrain that night."

"No. I could just tell you had a lot going on. And I'd be lying if I said I wasn't curious, but I don't ask nosy questions because I kind of can't stand it when people do it to me."

"Oh, I wasn't going to ask." Shrugging, she says, "I know your type. I assumed you lost your leg in a circus accident. You're a lion tamer, am I right?"

I laugh so hard that I'm damn near choking. "Close, but not quite. Guess again."

"Slipped while climbing Mount Everest?"

"Nope."

"Shark attack off the Great Barrier Reef?"

"I wish. That'd be a much better story to tell."

She looks at the t-shirt I'm wearing, zeroing in on the small skull insignia with IYAOYAS written underneath. "Armed forces?"

"Navy. And, yeah, the leg was a casualty of war." I don't want her pity, even though she doesn't seem like the type who'd go all sappy and sympathetic on me, but I laugh it off just in case she's about to go heading down that road. "It happened during a routine recon mission...Boring story."

"Yep," she nods, "you're a dime a dozen. If I were you I'd lie when people asked me. I'd say it was a snake bite that got infected while you were stranded in the desert after your plane went down or something."

"You're pretty good at coming up with stories on the fly, aren't you?"

"Years of practice, I guess."

She finishes her water and then goes to stand up. I'm sitting there trying to figure out what she meant by that last comment, that is, if she meant anything at all, but the sight of her on full display erases pretty much everything else from my brain.

I stand when she does and then gesture for her to leave the plates. "I'll get this."

"Ok, thanks. I'm heading inside to change. See you in a bit."

"She's off limits, my friend. Believe me, I've tried."

I turn to see Leo's friend Max eyeing Grace as she makes her way across the yard and inside. I've met him a few times, and while he can come off as an ass sometimes, my gut tells me he's basically a good guy.

"How are you, Max?"

"You know me...Looking for love in all the wrong places."

That earns him a laugh. "I thought you were serious with that girl, the nurse. What was her name?"

"Nadia." He shakes his head. "We broke up a couple of weeks ago."

"Sorry to hear it. She seemed like a good person."

"She was. I mean, she is. I screwed that up and she's not the type to put up with my shit. My mother says I self-sabotage."

"Your *mom*?"

He laughs and then takes a sip of his drink. "She's a clinical psychologist. And she's right. When things start getting serious I do something to fuck it up. In this case, I did Nadia's friend, Lexi."

"Jesus. I'm glad she kicked your ass to the curb."

"It was fully deserved." He tilts his beer in the direction

that Grace just headed. "And even if that one wasn't already spoken for, Skylar would put a hit out on me if I so much as spoke to any one of her friends."

"I guess she knows your act."

"She certainly does."

I keep Grace's current status to myself, just in case Max does go getting any ideas where she's concerned. And then I smile to myself, repeating the line my own mother throws out like confetti whenever the chips are down: *Always remember that something good is right around the corner.*

Something good.

I'm hoping that's Grace.

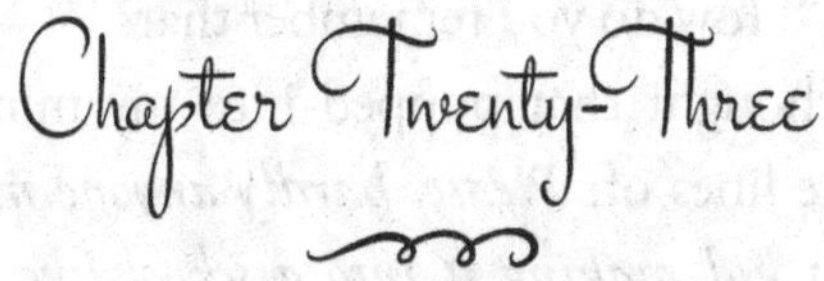

# Chapter Twenty-Three

## GRACE

Sitting upright, I rub the sleep from my eyes and take in my surroundings. Right, I crashed at Skylar and Leo's. Massaging my scalp, I remember those birthday shots that made my decision to stay over a no-brainer. I don't know what got into me last night.

Oh, yes I do.

Charlotte Mason.

When Skylar asked Sienna to fill her in on all the hometown gossip, she slapped her forehead and then looked over to where Garth was standing at the edge of the garden with their son. "I cannot believe I forgot to tell you!" Sienna looked to me when she asked, "Do you remember Simon Wade? He was in our year."

"Sure, he was in Honors English."

Skylar sighed, shaking her head. "So not fair. He was smart *and* hot."

Nodding, Sienna agreed, "Every girl had a crush on him. Anyway, Garth stays in touch with him. Not too often, but they talk on the phone from time to time."

"He was headed off to Northwestern, wasn't he?"

Sky asked, "How do you remember that?"

The first thought that popped into my mind was something along the lines of: *Please, hardly anyone makes it out of that town, so a kid making it into a school like Northwestern sticks out in your mind*, but I'd never say something so rude. Skylar made it out, despite a road that was long and bumpy, and Sienna and Garth are settled there and happy about it. Who am I to judge? Instead, I said, "Northwestern is no joke *and* he was a particularly good writer. He wrote poems, short stories..."

Sienna laughed. "I would have killed for a poem from that broody jerk back then, but alas, he just wasn't into me."

Sky poked her sister. "So what's the dirt?"

"Oh! So you remember when he was seeing Charlotte Mason towards the end of senior year?"

Sky nodded. "She was such a cutie."

And that's when I reached for the tequila bottle and poured a little something to steady myself.

Not the best day for a trip down memory lane. I was already feeling a little blue, what with it being my birthday and feeling like my feet have been set in concrete for the past couple of years. Add to that the plethora of happy couples and young families at this shindig. It was only four or five couples and three families, but still, I was comparing my lonely life to those more fortunate. God, I was making myself sick with the sad sack routine.

Lost in my own head, I still caught the basics: Simon was

already more than halfway through law school and Charlotte was a junior at University of Michigan. But I perked up when Sky put her hand to her chest, eyes wide. "He's *how* old?"

Sienna nodded. "Right? I couldn't believe it either. Simon was always looking for her, and all that time, Charlotte was just a few hours away raising their baby by herself."

Then *I* was the one with my hand to my chest, eyes wide and finding it hard to breathe. "What?"

Sienna said, "She had a baby. His name is Ethan. I think he's four? Anyway, they're together now."

Olivia came over at that very moment, situated herself on my lap and reached up to curl her fingers into my hair. What normally felt awkward and unwanted was now something I needed.

*A baby. I knew she was pregnant.*

Skylar was thinking out loud when she said, "Wow, she left school because she was pregnant," and then looked to her sister again. "How did they reconnect?"

"I don't know the details," Sienna said, "but I do know that Simon was in the dark up until pretty recently."

Dragging my ass over to the fridge in the pool house to get myself some much needed water, I replay the conversation in my head. Charlotte Mason. What was she, fifteen or sixteen at the time? Uneasy, maybe, but she didn't flinch that day when I called her down to my classroom. A girl with a spine made of steel.

I was four years older than her when I found myself peeing on a stick, my heart racing as I waited for those faint lines that would determine my future.

I was a coward.

I still am.

I remember looking away, blinking back tears last night, only to see that guy Owen looking right back at me. His eyes were searching and kind, like maybe he somehow knew I was struggling. So I did my best to shake it off and then pasted on my winning smile like I always do, but damn, I was exhausted.

*No more*, I thought to myself last night. *I'm not doing this anymore.*

And if I'd had just one more shot I might have spilled my sob story to Skylar, Sienna, and to anyone else who happened to be within earshot.

Thank God I had the sense to excuse myself. I slipped out back, curled up on a sofa in the pool house and drifted off to sleep dreaming of what could have been.

*My bag, my keys.*

Fixing my hair into a topknot and then looking down to make sure the sundress I wore yesterday is in place and covering my goodies the way it should be, I'm hoping that I can just slip into the kitchen, grab my stuff and make a quick getaway.

"Aunt Grace! Can I have a dance lesson today?"

Right, little kid on the premises. The house is up and buzzing.

Sky looks at me and then smirks as she pours syrup over a plate of pancakes, Olivia is alternating between dancing in circles and playing with my birthday present, and Leo is sitting at the kitchen table with some guy I don't know and one that I definitely do.

"Morning, Grace."

Owen's eyes stay on me as Leo introduces their friend—can't recall his name—and then Leo adds, "Were you able to sleep out there? It can get really hot."

I absently reach up to touch my head, sure that my unruly curls are springing out in several different directions as we speak. A finger comb-through doesn't cut it with hair like mine.

"Yeah...Um, hi."

That's all I manage to get out before Olivia grabs my hand and drags me into the living room. She's dressed in one of the sparkly tutus I got for her last birthday and pleading with me to watch as she gets herself into a pretty comical imitation of first position.

I'm aware that he's still watching me as I set Olivia's arms properly and adjust her feet so they're parallel. "Perfect," I tell her, stepping back. My cheeks are flushed.

She holds it for all of a nanosecond before breaking into a wild dance that doesn't follow the rhythm of whatever Skylar's got playing on the speaker.

I look to Skylar. "That's how kids *should* dance. Holding your body in those rigid positions at her age is torture."

"Oh, I have no intention of going the dance mom route. She likes dancing this week, last week it was jewelry making, next week it'll be cake decorating."

"Or fixing cars," Leo says.

She nods as she sets a big platter onto the table. "Or fixing cars. My point is, if she wants to dance it's going to be the kind of lessons Sienna and I took with that lady at the community center. It was pure fun, not crazy or competitive."

"I loved ballet, but I can't say I ever felt like I was having fun at the studio." Grabbing my bag off the counter, I add, "Miss Abramov was half drill sergeant, half pitbull."

Owen catches my eye. "That sounds awful."

I can laugh at the memory now. "You have no idea. I just hope she's not terrorizing the next generation of young dancers."

As they start filling their plates with scrambled eggs and

pancakes, I take the opportunity to split. "The party was great, and thank you so much for the present and the beautiful cake." Looking to Olivia, I add, "You made my day super special."

"Can't you stay for breakfast?" Leo asks.

"No." Backing up towards the door, I make some lame excuse about having lots to do, then wave and say goodbye to the group before bolting.

I catch my breath once I'm out the door, pausing with my hand still resting on the doorknob. What *was* that? I try to chalk the weirdness up to the after effects of a slight hangover, but nope, I feel just fine. Owen is attractive, but I've been around plenty of good looking guys without spazzing before, so that's not it either.

He's into me, that's it.

Owen looks at me like he's trying to figure me out, and I don't know how I feel about being the subject of someone's scrutiny.

Yeah, that vow I made last night, the whole *I'm not doing this hiding thing anymore*? Right now I want nothing more than to be back in the quiet sanctuary of Aunt Viv's house.

I'm just starting towards my car when the door opens and Owen steps outside. "Grace, wait up."

I take a breath to shore myself up and then turn to him. "Hey."

"Hey. I thought you left last night. Didn't realize you were camped out in the pool house."

"Did you crash here, too?"

"No." He shakes his head smiling and then gestures down the street. "I live a few blocks that way and around the corner."

"Nice."

There's a pause before he says, "I was wondering if you'd like to go out sometime." And with his hands jammed into his pockets, he's looking a little bit nervous and a lot cute. "You know, like grab dinner or something?" Before I can answer, he says, "I know you just got out of something serious, so if it's too soon just say the word. I'll understand."

It's been what, a week, ten days? It is too soon. But looking down at my feet, trying to hide what's surely written on my face, I know that I want to say yes. Fuck it, I like him.

"I'll go out with you." And then I look up to meet his eyes, feeling more sure about what I'm setting into motion. "I'd like that."

Owen looks relieved. "Good." He smiles and cocks his head to the side before saying, "Any chance you're free tomorrow or the day after?" When I let out a surprised laugh, he adds, "It's just that I'm going away for a week and I don't want to wait that long to see you."

"You're a *go big or go home* kind of guy, aren't you?"

"You could say that."

"Where are you going?"

"Just to New York. I have to be in the city for a few days."

"Nice. I used to love visiting New York with my parents when I was a kid."

"Same here." He fixes his eyes on mine, expectant.

"I'm free tomorrow night. But I live like an hour away from here."

He hands me his phone. "Put your number and your address in. I'll come to you."

"Are you sure? I'm not exaggerating when I say that the nightlife is lacking."

"I could care less."

"Then it's a date."

He opens my car door for me, and I think I must be

wearing the same goofy smile he's sporting. "See you tomorrow, Grace."

And in that moment, I suddenly feel like little Olivia, jumpy and impatient. I've got lots to do, and I can't wait for tomorrow.

# Chapter Twenty-Four

OWEN

I'm curious more than anything else when I pull into the driveway, looking down at my phone again to make sure I've got the right address.

Grace lives in a house, a small ranch. I was expecting an apartment, something more suited to a person our age. I mean, I own my own home, but most people our age don't go down that road until after they walk down the aisle.

I take in the cracks on the concrete porch, the faded curtains hanging in the front windows, and the flowering shrubs that look like they're in serious need of some tender loving care.

Grace dresses like a cross between a Hollywood starlet and a high-end fortune teller. She's all about color, bangles and beads. This place is the polar opposite. The weather-beaten pale green siding looks like it was installed thirty years ago.

I'm about to knock when I hear music coming from the backyard, so I walk around instead. Grace is shaking her hips to some pop music as she sets the patio table with a bright blue tablecloth, sunshine yellow napkins and some colorful plates in a Talavera design. This is more like it.

"Oh, hey!"

"Sorry to sneak up on you like that. I was about to knock until I heard the music on back here."

She walks over to lower the volume on the speaker. "You're early." She looks pleased when she says it, though, which puts me at ease. "Are those for me?" she asks, looking at the bunch of flowers I'm holding. "I love tiger lilies. Orange is one of my favorite colors."

"You seem more the tiger lily type than, I don't know, plain old roses ."

"For future reference, I like roses too. The only flowers I don't like are mums and gladiola. They remind me of funerals." Looking back over her shoulder, she says, "Come on in so I can find a vase for these."

"How long have you lived here?" I ask as I look around. The brown shag carpet, the flowered sofa and loveseat—everything screams senior citizen.

She follows the path my eyes are taking. "My Aunt Vivian left the house to me. I couldn't bring myself to move in at first, but I've been here for," she pauses to think, "nine months now." Her smile drops when she adds, "I know it needs a lot of work, but I just can't seem to get started. All of my furniture is still in storage."

"I didn't take you for a brown paneling kind of girl."

She winces and then laughs. "It's vintage, you fool." Still looking around the kitchen for a vase, she says, "This place is still like a shrine to Aunt Viv. I've thought about doing a whole remodel and redecorate, but..."

I pick up where she trails off. "That would mean you're

setting down roots. You said you wanted to leave your job...Maybe you're looking to make some other big changes, too."

"This will have to do," she says as she rinses out an old mason jar. And it's not lost on me that she ignored that last comment I made. Too personal. I make a mental note to keep things on the light side.

"Can I get you a beer, a glass of wine?"

"Wine sounds good."

"I only have red. Is that all right?"

"I only drink red so it's perfect."

She pours us both a glass. "I went to France last summer and had a case of my favorite wine shipped back home. I've been hoarding it."

"I'm honored you're opening a bottle of the good stuff for me." Taking a sip, I let it sit there on my tongue for a few seconds before swallowing. "This is good."

"I was there with my boyfriend but he was busy with work stuff, so I signed up for a cooking class in Paris, took a ferry out to Mont Saint-Michel, and," she clinks her glass to mine, "I toured a few vineyards in Bordeaux."

Now I know for certain that her ex is a bonehead. "Did you see *any* of the sights with him?"

"We spent one day at the Louvre. He had a conference to attend and then he was busy doing detailed research on Voltaire and Rousseau. He's big into French Enlightenment philosophers." She pauses then adds, "It was never sold to me like a romantic getaway. I knew from the start that I was tagging along on a work trip. But," she looks up at me, "eating alone in a restaurant is no fun."

"I bet."

My mind conjures up an image of Grace sitting alone in a

bistro, eating some of the best food on earth with no one to share the experience. It's a lonely image, one that makes my heart sink.

I've only been in this girl's presence a few times, but still, it's not the first time she's said or done something that's made me feel sad on her behalf. I remind myself again that this is a first date, to lighten up.

"I went to France and Belgium on a high school trip way back when. I'd like to get back there some day."

She nods and smiles. "Bruges is on my bucket list."

"You'd love it. It's like a city stuck in time, like you're walking through some fairytale. And I just remember the food being so incredibly good. Every single meal was like the best thing I'd ever tasted. I think my mother was offended when I came home and wouldn't stop talking about the food. I mean, she's a good cook, but they can make a chicken taste like—"

"Heaven, right?" She takes a sip of her wine, nodding. "The best roast chicken I'll probably ever have." Her eyes close like she's trying to get back there when she licks her lips and then says, "Oh, and those croissants..."

I'm staring at her now, thinking that I want to feed her a croissant, want to taste wine from her lips, want to sit in a café beside her and watch people walk by as we sip our morning coffee after a lazy morning in bed.

I want.

"Owen?" She waves a hand in front of my face, laughing. "I'm glad I'm not the only space cadet in town."

"Sorry."

"I was just saying you'll be able to score some great croissants in New York."

"Probably, but you've got me thinking about food,

woman. And now I want the real thing…A buttery croissant in Paris."

"Well, tonight you'll have to do with my best stab at Moroccan. I made lamb tagine." She says this as she's lifting a clay pot out of the oven.

"Something exotic, I should have guessed."

This makes her crack up. "I'm about the farthest thing from exotic."

"Exotic is in the eye of the beholder, or whatever that saying is. Can I help you?"

"Grab our plates from outside and we'll serve ourselves in here, ok?"

"I'm on it."

We head back out, plates piled high with couscous and stewed lamb, but she's swatting at her ankles inside of two minutes.

"Let's go back inside. The mosquitoes are eating you alive."

"Do you mind? It's so nice out tonight but the bugs *are* getting a little pesky." She passes as I hold the back door open for her. "They used to attack Aunt Viv, too. She'd tell me they only like the sexy people."

"She sounds like she was a pretty funny lady."

"She was like a warm hug personified. Viv never had children, which is a shame. She would have made a great mother."

We eat in comfortable silence for the next few minutes, with me sitting there thinking to myself that I do indeed like Moroccan food.

"This is delicious, Grace."

"I'm so glad you like it. I took some up to Sky and Leo's for a pot-luck they had last fall and Olivia devoured it. She's the only five-year-old I know who'd eat this."

"I think she'd eat a shoe if you were the one cooking it."

Grace looks amused when I tell her, "I couldn't help but notice at the party that she's really attached to you."

She covers her mouth with her napkin, laughing. "She is but I have no idea why."

"Libs looks at you like you're a rock star or something."

"I think it's just a dance phase kind of thing."

"A dancer, huh? Yeah, you looked like you were hard core when you were showing her the moves."

She shakes her head and waves me off. "I bailed out of the ballet world when I was fourteen. I *did* minor in dance theory back in college, but I don't consider myself a dancer."

"What did you want to do with your degree?"

She shrugs. "Exactly what I am doing, I guess. I teach English literature and creative writing, and I coach our high school dance team." She pauses then adds, "I do love certain aspects of my job, but I feel restless lately. I can't really put my finger on why that is."

"Did you grow up here?"

"Philly."

"Not like this is so far from there, but—"

"But at the same time, it's worlds away. I know. It's just that I needed a safe place to land after college and Aunt Viv was my safe place. My parents got divorced when I was in high school, they both remarried, and their new houses never felt like home." Grace tilts her head to the side. "Are your parents still married?"

"Nearly forty years and still going strong."

"That's awesome. And you're from where?"

"Pittsburgh...The burbs."

She lays her fork down, rests her elbows on the table and perches her chin on her hands. "So?"

"What?"

"So tell me your life story, Owen. You're on your second glass of wine. Maybe I'll get some secrets out of you this time."

"I guess that's only fair." I rub my hands together. "All right. I grew up the oldest of three kids. I have two younger sisters. I went to the Naval Academy, served two tours overseas, came home missing an appendage."

She laughs at that line and I'm oddly grateful for her sick sense of humor.

"I was going to study law but decided against it. I love reading and writing about history, so teaching seemed like a natural fit."

"What else?"

"What do you mean?"

"Hmm...What do you want?"

And I know what she's asking me, but I'm not sure how much I want to reveal. Grace isn't the stereotype people like to draw of women in their mid-thirties. She's obviously not desperate to get married. Looking down at my plate, I get the feeling that she'd rather ride a camel around Marrakech than settle down in a house like mine—picket fence and all that goes with it.

"What do I want?" I sit on the question for a moment. "I'm pretty simple. And I have most of the things I've always wanted. My job makes me happy, I have friends I enjoy spending time with, I have a house..." I study her face for a moment, wondering if I should go there. Fuck it. She asked so I'm going to answer. If she doesn't like the answer, it's better to know where she stands now before I go setting myself up for a let-down. "My house feels empty, though. Like it's waiting for me to fill it up or something."

"With a houseful of kids?"

I shake my head and laugh, even though I'm thinking

something along the lines of: *One or two kids would do.* "At this point, I'd settle for a woman."

"Your last woman wasn't on board with your life plan?"

I shrug because I have no idea what Ava was on board with. All I know is that she was not the one.

"I actually dated her back in high school. Our families are close, parents are good friends and all that. It was nothing serious. We went to the prom together and then that was it. I left for college, was away for the better part of a decade. We didn't reconnect until last year. Ava was divorced from her husband by that time and, I don't know, she's always been around." I laugh, knowing how ridiculous I sound. "That's obviously not a good reason to start a relationship with someone."

"Agreed."

She tops our glasses off, leaving the bottle empty.

"My parents used to call an empty wine bottle a dead soldier."

Grace winces. "That's a terrible saying."

"They stopped once I signed on for Annapolis."

"I'll bet. What made you choose the Naval Academy?"

"My grandfather was a Marine and he was a big influence in my life."

"Your father, too?"

"No. He didn't serve. I think my grandfather judged him for that, and maybe I did too for a while there. I ate up everything my grandfather told me about battle and sacrifice and all that."

"It is a huge sacrifice."

"But it's a choice. No one forces you anymore. And I don't judge people one way or the other. That life isn't for everyone."

"Would you do it all over again?"

I don't have to think about it before answering, "Absolutely. I don't have any regrets." I smile, adding, "Maybe I would have taken a different route that last day. You know, avoided that bomb planted along the roadside. But other than that..."

Grace's eyes sparkle when she laughs. Add that to the long list of things I like about her.

"Have you always had a sense of humor about what happened to you?" She asks as I get up to clear the table. "Leave those in the sink. I'll get them later," she tells me as I start to run the water.

"Nope. You cooked, I clean."

She moves in close, drops the utensils into the soapy water and then teases, "Sucks for you then...No dishwasher in this dump."

I hip check her snarky ass. "I'll manage. And to answer your question, I've always at least tried to have a sense of humor about it. A lot of men came back worse off than I did."

"Or didn't come back at all," she whispers.

"Exactly."

I turn around when she doesn't say anything more. She looks lost in thought as she's uncorking another bottle of wine.

I've had two glasses, not much, but if I'm driving an hour back home tonight then I have to watch it. I grab another glass and fill it from the faucet, downing it in one go.

She takes our two glasses and walks into the living room, setting them on the coffee table. I'm edgy as I dry the last of the dishes, knowing that we're approaching that awkward turning point in our night. Heading to the couch to join her, I'm hoping this goes the way I want.

"You don't mind that we stayed in and ate here, do you? I just realized that I kind of took over, but the fine dining options around here are limited to a mediocre diner and a sub shop."

"Not at all. Dinner was great."

"Thank you."

"I'll cook for you next time."

She side-eyes me as she sips her wine. "Why do I have this feeling that you're some master chef or something?"

"I have absolutely no idea. And I definitely don't want to disappoint you, but when I said cook for you I meant grill you a burger."

She laughs. "Well, you know I like burgers."

I rest my head back on the couch, close my eyes and sigh to tease her when I say, "Watching you eat a cheeseburger was the highlight of my week."

She surprises me when she shoots back, "That's how you know a man likes sex...When he actually gets off on the sight of a woman eating."

I nearly spit my wine out at that one, and it takes me a full minute to stop laughing. "You've met a guy who doesn't like sex?"

She tilts her head to the side and shrugs in a way that's playful and so damn sexy. "You know what I mean...Some like it more than others."

# Chapter Twenty-Five

GRACE

I went there.

I brought sex into the conversation and now the air is thick with tension. Not the bad kind. No, the air is crackling with uncertainty and anticipation. We're at that point where one of us is either going to push us over the edge, or the moment will pass and slip into that big black hole of regrets and missed opportunities.

When he looks to me with a question in his eyes, my body heats. I haven't been touched the way I need to be touched in a very long time, and right now I'm downright aching for Owen.

He sets his down glass on the table and then takes mine and does the same. "Come here," he says, taking one of my hands and gesturing for me to move onto his lap. The casual slip of a dress I'm wearing rides up my thighs as I move to straddle him, and the friction of his jeans against my skin has me burning with a need to move. I want to push my chest up against his and slide in even closer so that I can feel him between my legs.

I want his hands on me.

Time does something to a woman. I still have insecurities, still have moments where I'm berating myself over the decisions I've made, but I certainly give less fucks than I did a decade ago. I don't feel ashamed to want this, to want a man I've spent hardly any time with. So when he pauses with his hands holding both sides of my face, I don't feel the least bit shy when I tell him that I want him to touch me.

He keeps his hands on my face, though, pulls me in gently and kisses me. And for a moment there I forget about my needy self, because his kiss and the way his hands are cradling my face make me feel so cherished and adored that I have to hold back the emotion. *He doesn't even know you*, I tell myself. *You're substituting him for someone he's not.*

And then my body is back on fire. Whoever or whatever this is, I don't care. I want and I will take whatever he's offering.

Owen stops and pulls back, hands still on my face. "Hey, where'd you go?"

It takes a moment to register, takes a moment to open my eyes and really see him. "What do you mean?"

"Are you here with *me*, Grace?" Hands back resting on my hips, he looks off to the side when he says, "I know it was pretty forward to ask you out a week after you broke off your engagement. Maybe that wasn't fair to you."

"I'm not thinking about him, I promise."

"You look sad, though."

"I'm just...I've gone without for a long time." He cocks his head to the side. "Not without sex," I clarify. "Without feeling anything when I'm close to someone. I know that sounds awful." I scoot my hips back. "Maybe I am still a bit of a mess over it. Staying with him all this time because it was safe and easy…"

"Doesn't make you a terrible person. Now if you married the guy and didn't really love him, that's a different story."

"You look at me and I feel…"

"What?"

"Desired?"

His smile is soft as he drags my hips back in. "I desire you, Grace. I've made no secret of that."

I breathe in deep when I feel him pressed up against me. He wants me, I'm sure of that, and I need him.

Unable to meet his eyes, I look down at the buttons on the bodice of my dress and set about undoing them slowly. "Do we have to hash it all out tonight then? I don't want to talk about my past or your past. I don't have to know everything there is to know about you just yet. I just know that I want you."

He tips my chin up so that we're eye to eye, then brushes my fingers aside as he takes over the task of undressing me. "Yeah, we can leave the talking for some other time."

When he moves the fabric down my shoulders and I'm bared to him from the waist up, I'm mentally patting myself on the back for forgoing the bra. He eyes stay fixed there as he whispers, "Holy fuck, Grace."

Taking his hands in mine, I lead him there, guide him to cup me with both hands. When his thumbs brush over me, my head rolls back as I struggle to hold in the primal moan building inside of me. And then his head is between my breasts, his warm breath skating over my skin before he latches onto me, sucking, licking and kissing me in a way that has me squirming and desperate to get closer.

"Here," he says, taking the fabric of my dress from around my hips and lifting it up and over my head. Tossing it aside, he looks me over and says to no one in particular, "I've been dreaming about this body for weeks."

"Weeks?"

"Yeah. Couldn't take my eyes off you the first night I met you," he kisses my jaw as his hands squeeze the flesh on my hips, "and then seeing you wearing hardly anything at all the other day," he pauses again to circle his tongue around one aching nipple, "I've been dreaming about fucking you."

That moan I was holding back? It tears out from somewhere deep inside of me when he wedges a hand between us, slips beneath the lace and lands between my legs. "Owen."

"You feel so good."

"Want you," I whisper as I roll my hips to press against his hand.

He kisses me, uses his free hand to tease my tits, tongues my mouth like he's fucking me for real, and has me coming inside of two minutes. "So good," he whispers as he keeps his hand there, waiting for my body to come down from the high.

My heart is pounding long after my breath evens out, and my cheeks are flushed. I can't look at him yet, so I reach down between us and pop the button on his jeans instead, whispering, "Now you."

He tips my chin up again, and his soft smile erases any trace of the awkwardness I was feeling just a moment before. "This bumpy couch isn't going to do it for me. I need to get you in a bed."

And I want to smack my own forehead in that moment, as it occurs to me for the first time that there are probably some logistics involved in this for Owen.

I stand, and he uses the armrest for leverage to get himself up off the marshmallow-like cushions of Viv's thirty-year-old couch.

With my hand held out for him to take, wearing hardly anything all, I like the way he's looking at me. He likes what he sees, and although I know this is lust more than anything else, he makes me feel beautiful.

He takes my hand and kisses it before following me into the bedroom. And I'm thanking the stars up above that I did at least swap out Viv's old bedroom set for mine—her old chenille bedspread may have been a deal breaker. Still, nothing of mine hangs on the walls and the floor is bare. I watch as his eyes scan the room, as he takes in the crocheted afghan folded over the back of the rocking chair and the collection of figurines that still sits on the shelf. It hits home harder than ever before that I've been stuck these past few years, wasting time, one foot in the present and one in my shadowed past.

Looking to hide in the darkness, I reach for the bedside lamp but Owen turns me back around to face him. "No, baby. I need to see you and you need to see me."

He tugs the shirt up over his head and then holds my eyes when he stands in front of me and pushes his jeans over his hips and down. He wants me to acknowledge who he is, and it's not lost on me that I'm being tested. Owen is strong, proud and confident. I knew that right off the bat. He doesn't want my pity, but when he sits down across from me to finish taking off his jeans and then stands again, my heart sinks for the young man who endured all that pain.

"What do you see?"

"The first time I met you I tagged you as some preening dude...All ego. You know, the ones who spend entirely too much time working out?" He smiles at this. "Your suit was fitted just so, cut to show off the build underneath the clothing. The super-clean shave, your hair, the clothes...I figured you had a really high opinion of yourself. Not that there's anything wrong with self-love, but I dismissed you as being one of those guys who just *loves* the mirror. But then at the party when I saw your leg, I realized that you *have* to be strong. I saw that six pack of yours in a different light." I reach out to touch his hand, a gesture to bring him closer to me where I'm sitting on the bed. "Strength and determination, that's what I see when I look at you."

Looking up at him, I tug the snug cotton fabric over his ass and down. Owen doesn't stop me when I stroke him, so I take that as a green light and lick him from base to tip. And I like it when he places a commanding hand on my head, leading me gently while taking control. He groans when I skate my fingernails over his ass, but he must be getting close because that's when he puts the brakes on.

"Good?" I ask him.

"Too good...I just don't want this to end." He gestures for me to lie back on the bed and asks, "Are you on anything?"

"Yeah, I'm set."

I saw him place a condom on the nightstand before he took his jeans off, and now I watch, perched up on my elbows as he rolls it over and down his cock. "I'm so ready," I tell him as I push my underwear down and then toss it aside. "How do you want me?"

"Just like that," he says, but he walks around to the other side of the bed and when he climbs on, he rolls me to my side so that I'm facing away from him.

I need him to take the lead, to show me how to do this and make it good for him. But once he moves in close, the thinking stops and the feeling begins. His muscled body pressed up against my back, his dick against my ass, his free hand roaming over my hips and my tits—I am on fire. My breaths are coming in ragged as I arch back and rub myself against him.

He whispers in my ear, "Gonna fuck you so good," as he enters me for the first time, and I gasp when he hits me deep. Over and over and over. His thrusts are punishing but his caresses are gentle. And his words are just what I need to throw me over the edge again.

Still inside me, he leans in close and nuzzles the skin below my ear. "Even better than my fantasies, and those were pretty damn hot."

"God, I needed that."

"At your service, Grace. I'll report for duty anytime." Owen shifts when I laugh, and then rolls me onto my back so that I'm looking up at him. "Really, that was *so* good. Thank you."

"Hmm...I've never been thanked for sex before."

He knows I'm teasing, though, and squeezes my ass when he shoots back, "Well, I'm still waiting on a thank you for my fancy finger work back there on the couch. I'm starting to think you're kinda rude."

"Then merci beaucoup. That *was* pretty fantastic."

He grabs a tissue from the nightstand and gets up to get rid of the condom. I watch him, quiet though my head is filled with questions.

"Can you stay?"

I don't even know where that came from. I was floating different sorts of questions. *Did I do it right? Are there positions that are off limits? Do you usually leave your prosthetic on?* Too soon for all that, I know. And now I'm turning crimson, figuring that I just came off sounding hella needy. Asking him to stay over on the first date, hookup, or whatever this is?

"Uh, it's just that you had some wine, so I don't want you to feel—"

"Yeah, I'll stay." He turns back to me and smiles. "I'd like that."

# Chapter Twenty-Six

## OWEN

It wasn't a dream.

I'm content when I hear the sound of steady breathing beside me, feel her soft naked skin nestled up against mine, and my drowsy eyes open and take in my surroundings. I'm in Grace's bed. A voice inside my head decides: *This is good.*

I roll onto my side, wrap my free arm around her body and then breathe her in. Grace, the sheets, the room—the sweet smell of good loving is in the air. I shift to get closer still, and in that moment I'm reminded that my leg is off.

She asked me last night, laying side by side after our second outstanding session, if I kept my prosthetic on when I slept. "No," I told her, but the truth is that I was contemplating keeping it on before she asked the question.

People make a point of commenting on what they perceive as resilience in the face of adversity, my self-confidence, my fearless, can-do attitude. And that's the face I show to the world—most days. I am disabled, but I'm not weak and I never wan't to be perceived that way. And while I would say that I have a positive self-image overall, I'll admit to moments of doubt, self-pity and even shame.

I didn't want to take my leg off in front of Grace last night. It's inevitable, that is, if she does want to see me again and get to know me better. But last night I wanted to be a man in her eyes—complete and whole and able.

I forced her to watch as I bared myself to her. It wasn't some big reveal, she already knew, but I needed to see her face, to see if she wanted me the way a woman wants a man in her bed. And thank God I only saw longing as Grace's eyes roamed up and over me.

*Some preening dude. You know, the ones who spend entirely too much time working out?*

I smile thinking back to that wiseass comment, her first impression of me. And I was grateful for those hours spent in the gym when she raked her eyes over every inch of my body. *You have to be strong*, she said, and she got that right. It's not a choice for me. My abs need to be solid to keep me steady and balanced, and my arms, chest and shoulders need to be able to bear an insane amount of weight just so that I can move and get through the activities of daily living that everyone else takes for granted.

Bottom line is that Grace wanted me, and sex with her was so much better than I ever could have hoped for. Round two had her riding me with her long hair falling down and over her breasts. She was like a living, breathing work of the most beautiful art.

I'm getting hard again just thinking back to what she said, her sexy words and whimpers. Grace is a woman who likes sex, and that's about the hottest thing in the world.

Her eyes flutter open, and then she smiles as if she's pleasantly surprised when she sees me. Maybe she thought she was dreaming, too.

"Good morning."

She stretches like a cat, back arched and arms up over her head. She's doesn't seem to care or notice that the sheets have slipped down below her breasts, and why should she? The woman's body is insane, and I'm so glad I'm getting another chance to admire it.

"Morning," she answers before covering her mouth. "Be right back," she says as she gets out of bed. "I don't want to kiss you with dragon breath."

I take the moment alone to put my leg on and then follow her into the bathroom once I hear the shower start up. As I'm flushing, I realize we probably don't know each other well enough for me to be doing my business while she's in the shower, but she doesn't bat an eye when she peeks out from behind the curtain to tell me, "I don't have an extra toothbrush but feel free to use mine if you're not grossed out by sharing."

"You sure?"

She giggles and then shoots me a look. "We swapped a lot more than saliva last night, so it's fine by me."

"This is true."

I take my time brushing because Grace's shower curtain is one of those sheer numbers where you can make out the silhouette of her form and watch as she moves. Shaking my head, I curse the fact that I can't join her. Shower sex used to be fun.

I sit on the bed and wait for her in my underwear, floating an idea that I'm pretty sure she'll shoot down. Grace comes out of the bathroom wrapped in a towel, looking so cute that I want to pull her onto my lap and repeat last night all over again.

"What's up?"

"Are you the spontaneous type or do you like things planned out in advance?"

She cocks her head to the side and then comes to sit next to me on the bed. "A little of both, I guess."

"Want to come to New York with me tomorrow?"

"You said you had plans. Would I be in the way?"

"No, I'd love it if you came with me. I have two days where I have shit to do, but I booked the hotel for four days because I'm off from work and I've got nothing else going on right now."

She nods her head but doesn't say anything for a full minute. She's probably weighing the pros and cons of going away with someone she barely knows. Normally I'd be doing the same, but I don't know, I have this feeling that Grace and I will come through this little adventure just fine.

"I could totally amuse myself for two days in New York."

"I'll only be tied up part of each day, so I'll be able to do stuff with you. You won't be on your own." I want to add: *Not like when you were in Paris with that douchebag.*

"Do you mind me asking what you're doing up there?"

I take her hand just because I want the contact, and also to convey that it's all right to ask. I want her to know everything there is to know. "I have to get an MRI done tomorrow afternoon and then I have a consultation with an orthopedic surgeon the next day."

"For your leg?"

I nod down at it. "There's a more advanced procedure. It's not really new but there aren't many hospitals that specialize in it. It's called osseointegration limb replacement. The prosthetic is surgically implanted into the bone, as opposed to mine, which is a more traditional socket-base prosthetic."

"You must be going to HSS then." I must look surprised because she shrugs, adding, "My parents are both physicians and so is my brother. No orthopedists in the family, but hospital talk was like background noise growing up in my house."

I'm kind of thrown for a moment there. The Hansons aren't exactly a family of slouches, but having three doctors in one family is crazy impressive. "Wow."

"Yep, a family of geniuses with one exception."

I knock her knee with my good one. "Don't go busting on teachers."

"I'm not," she nudges me back. "I just usually hold back on telling people about my family. I come off like the square peg."

"I get it. And yeah, that's where I'm going. I don't even know if I'm a good candidate for it or not, but it could be an interesting option."

"What's the worst thing about it?" She's looking down at my foot so I know she's not asking about the surgery.

I rest back on my elbows and sigh, trying to make a joke of it. "About five minutes ago I wanted to join you in there," I nod towards the bathroom, "but I didn't have my shower leg with me. Basically, I need to travel with a duffel bag of assorted attachments. Got my shower leg, my running leg, my walking leg..."

She gestures for me to scoot back and then moves to straddle me. "And this doesn't hurt? You didn't complain last night, but I'm not exactly a waif."

She's bare, pressed up against me where I want her. "No," I tell her, and suddenly I'm struggling to remember what it is that she asked me. Her eyes are knowing, and she continues to tease me when she slowly tugs at the towel she's wearing and looks down between us as it falls to the floor.

Coming back to my senses, I ask her, "You don't seriously think this would hurt me, do you?"

She shakes her head. "You're a big boy. I know you can handle me."

Such a smart ass, and I fucking love it.

Grace lets out a happy scream when I toss her over and pin her beneath me. I can play her game, and while I liked that view, I don't always like being on the bottom. "I can handle you morning, noon and night," I whisper as I reach down to touch her, and I damn near growl when I feel how slick she is. "Give me one more, Grace," I plead as I push my underwear down and enter her, and then I'm lost.

I can hear her in the background, but then I dial back in so that I can really focus on her, on what she's telling me. How does she expect a man to last when she talks that way? Begging to be fucked, telling me to ride her harder? A mouth so wicked and so beautiful.

I want to fall at Grace's feet and worship her after I come. It's like she's feeding a man who's been starved of that intimate, good kind of loving for so long, and I don't ever want to go hungry again.

# Chapter Twenty-Seven

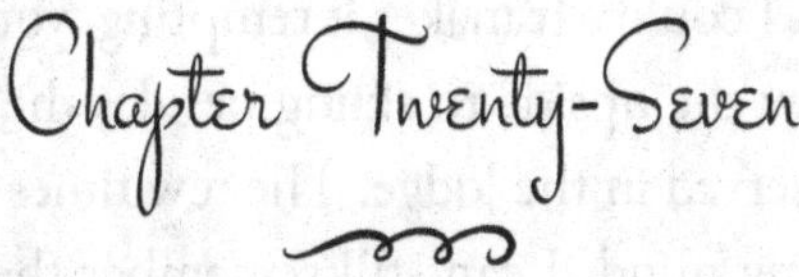

GRACE

"What did you think?"

We're walking down York Avenue holding hands, and I'm still kind of amazed that he even wanted me there with him. I know he thinks of me as different from a friend, but I like the friendship side of what's developing between us too.

*An extra set of ears always helps*, he told me, and I get it. What we just sat through was information overload. And I guess medicine is in my blood at least a teeny bit, because I did find all those cutting-edge advancements fascinating.

"It sounds like a no-brainer on the surface, right? Better control, better mobility. But then again, it's major surgery. There are risks."

"And the recovery and the rehab..."

"Are no joke."

"Exactly. Been under the knife enough times for this lifetime and another already. I'm not looking forward to another stint in the hospital." He gives my hand a gentle squeeze. "But I

207

have to admit, that video of the guy skiing has me seriously considering it."

"You used to ski?"

"No," he says before laughing. "But just knowing that if I *wanted* to then I could…It makes it tempting, you know?"

"I never saw the upside to skiing besides the hot chocolate and chili they served in the lodge. The few times I tried it I was scared out of my mind. I can still remember the sound of my skis skidding over patches of ice."

"Oh my," he teases. "You just physically shuddered. Was it that bad?"

"I remember careening out of control, falling on my ass, and it taking me forever just to untangle my skis and finally get off that mountain." I look up to him. "I mean hill…It was the bunny hill."

"No ski vacations, got it."

I tug on his hand and lead him down a side street to a café with outdoor seating. "This is more my speed."

"Is this the place with the best seafood salad in the universe?"

"So says the reviews."

"I could definitely eat."

"I've got someplace else picked out for dinner tomorrow night that you're going to love."

"You haven't steered me wrong so far. That falafel we got yesterday was insane. And I'll admit, I was doubting you when I saw the size of the place."

"If I went to NYU I would have lived on that stuff. Where else can you get lunch for four bucks in Manhattan, right?"

Once the waiter leaves us with bread and the wine we ordered, Owen says, "I feel like there's so much I still don't know about you." I look away, buttering a piece of bread as I think, *Oh, you have* no *idea.* "Where did you go to school?"

"Chapel Hill."

"Ah, I knew you were brainy."

"I didn't get into Duke, though. My parents' alma mater. It's where they met."

"Were they disappointed?"

"Yes, but seriously? If that's your biggest disappointment in life then I'd say you're batting a thousand."

"Absolutely."

"Did you like Annapolis?"

"Like it?" He looks down at the menu when he answers, "I can't answer yes or no to that. It's an experience, something that changes you...Hopefully for the better."

"I dated a Marine."

Now I've got his attention. "Really?"

I shake my head, waving it off. "Way back when."

I take a sip of my wine, hating myself for the way I've diminished Damien and what we had. I look back at the menu. "I'm getting the seafood salad, so you get something else and we'll share."

He doesn't say anything for a moment. I don't know Owen well, but I know enough to get that he's perceptive. I'm pretty sure he's reading into my words, my body language and my damn shaky breathing right now. But he lets me off the hook when he says, "Sounds good. I'll get the mushroom risotto."

Turning my head, I watch absently as people make their way to wherever they're going. I'm trying to close that door, to keep myself firmly planted in the present. But as I try in vain to come up with something to say, some witty diversion, a fatigue comes over me that's as familiar as it is troubling.

Damn, I promised myself I wouldn't do this anymore. No

more lies, no more hiding. Owen reaches across the small table at that moment and takes my hand in his, rubbing his thumb over my skin in a way that should be comforting but it's not.

I pull my hand from his when I blurt out, "I had a baby," and then suck in a breath as if I'm trying to retract that admission and lock it back up.

He reaches across again and gently lifts my chin. He nods once and calmly repeats what I just said, "You had a baby."

I nod, dumbstruck for a moment, and then realize what it is that I've done. "I'm sorry." I try to laugh even though I've got tears pooling at the corners of both eyes. "No one knows. It was a long time ago."

Owen tosses two twenties on the table and gestures to the waiter as he leads me out of the restaurant. We walk slowly in the direction of the hotel, saying nothing. In the elevator heading up to our room, Owen wraps an arm around my shoulder and whispers, "It's ok, Grace," as his lips graze the top of my head.

Owen said something the other day as we were walking through Central Park. I'd asked about his ex-girlfriend, again doing my best to keep the spotlight off myself, and he told me the basics. I got the feeling that his relationship with her was similar in some ways to mine with Jack: a situation you find yourself in more than something you choose.

When I asked how it ended, he said she'd lied to him. He told me about it, some ruse she'd concocted to get Owen to let her move in with him. He said he hated being lied to and he'd never trust her again after that. *Harsh*, I thought at the time. I honestly thought it was a pretty minor offense, a little white lie in the whole grand scheme of things. But I guess I'm partial to liars. They're my peeps.

He unlocks the door and I follow behind, my steps slow. I

imagined that saying those words out loud would lift a weight off my chest, but I don't feel so great at the moment.

"*Is* it ok?" I sit on the bed and look up at him. "I gave birth to a child. I gave her away. I never told anyone. You said you don't tolerate liars and I've been lying for years."

He pulls a chair over and sits opposite me. "Did you tell him?"

"He died before she was born."

"Aw, Gracie," he says as he pulls me in and holds me close. *Gracie*. I haven't been called that in years. And I know Owen isn't him, but he holds me the same way and speaks to me with the same tenderness in his voice. "It's gonna be all right."

It's a full five or ten minutes before I stop crying, before I pull back and see the front of his shirt soaked with my tears. My voice is hoarse when I whisper, "I'm sorry."

"Don't say that again. Don't apologize for telling me what's on your mind or in your heart."

He crosses the room to get me a bottle of water and some tissues. I try to stand but sit back down when I feel like I might just collapse. Lies are heavy, and I've been dragging them around for years and years.

Owen puts the bottle to my lips and then wipes my eyes. He sets the bottle down and then gets on the bed and gestures for me to crawl up and lie in the crook of his arm. When I do, he tucks me in beside him. He doesn't ask for details, doesn't push for more, and I'm grateful for it. He just strokes my hair, lulling me into a dreamless, deep sleep.

I wake up hours later, the room dark and the sun long past setting. My eyes feel swollen and there's an ache deep in my chest. I look over to see Owen on his back, his brow furrowed as he sleeps.

What was floating through his mind during my epic breakdown? Maybe he's thinking that I'm more than he bargained for. Maybe he's thinking Jack should be glad I let him off the hook. Maybe he's wishing this trip was over already. I know I am.

Telling the truth sucks.

He's awake when I come back in from the bathroom. "I fell asleep with this on," he says as he rests his prosthetic on the chair, "and I really shouldn't." When I don't say anything, he asks "Are you ok?"

"Aside from feeling massively embarrassed and uncomfortable? Yeah, I guess I'm ok."

"Can you pretend that you and me, that we're just friends? Can you trust in the idea that I won't judge you no matter what you tell me? I can't imagine holding something like that in for such a long time. It must hurt."

"This hurts worse."

"You said you've been lying for years but I don't see it that way."

"How?"

"To lie is to deceive someone on purpose. Who have you hurt besides yourself? You made a choice to bottle something painful up inside. It's entirely different."

"I paste a smile on my face every day. That smile is a lie. I have friends who have no idea who I am and don't know the single most important thing about me. My family doesn't know. I mean, I never told Jack and I was with him for years."

"Why didn't you tell Jack?"

I flop back down on my pillow and he gets back into bed leaving the space I need between us. "I don't know. I tried a few times but it never felt right. When we broke up he accused me of being in love with a ghost. I never told him much about Damien but he found some pictures, and he hated that I looked so happy in them. I never gave him the chance to know *that* girl. Jack should hate me. I wasted his time, I accepted his ring, and I never...Never once did I let him in."

"Sienna defended him that night when I called him an ass."

I'm confused for a moment. "At that faculty thing?"

"Yeah."

"Sienna's good-hearted, and I think she can see that Jack has always been knocking on a locked door. I think deep down he wanted to make me jealous that night." I let out a cheerless laugh. "He wanted me to react, to show some emotion. And he was massively disappointed when I simply didn't care."

"You didn't? I wanted to slap the shit out of him."

"I was relieved more than anything else. He gave me the out I was looking for. So that makes me a liar *and* a coward."

"You're neither."

"I hope he's with that grad assistant now."

I laugh when he says, "Me too." I look over to see him smiling at me. "I don't want him sniffing around you anymore."

"Oh," I drag my finger back and forth between us, "you still want this? Even now that you know I'm a hot mess?"

"Yeah, Grace," his smile drops. "I want this."

# Chapter Twenty-Eight

OWEN

Talk about a deep dive. That was the most intense getting to know you experience I've ever had, and that's saying a lot given the near-death experiences I've had in the company of people who were little more than strangers to me.

Grace is still shaky when we finally get up sometime around noon. We stayed up until dawn talking. She told me all about Damien, about finding out she was pregnant not long after he left, and then finding out he was dead all those months when she thought he'd abandoned her. My heart broke alongside hers when she told me about delivering the baby alone, twenty years old and scared out of her mind, and again when she told me about handing her baby over to the social worker, never to see her again.

I noticed the tattoo on the nape of her neck the other night in bed, but didn't bring it up. There was a date etched underneath the small bird, figured it was something personal and important to Grace. I figured right.

After she drifted off I stared up at the ceiling thinking about what she told me. I pictured the little tuft of black hair on her baby's head. Grace never knew babies were born with any hair, so she found herself running her fingers through it, amazed. She's called her Birdie since then, her little blackbird.

My eyes are tired and sad thinking about the strength women must possess to endure the things they do. Men are physically stronger in most cases, but women are sturdier in other ways.

"Can we do something mindless today?" she asks as she's pulling a shirt over her head. "No deep conversation, no drama," she's smiling when her heads pops out, "no crying?"

"It's our last day here. We'll do whatever you want."

"I want to go to The Metropolitan. I haven't been there in years. Ooh, and now they have a sculpture garden on the roof with a bar that's rumored to serve excellent mimosas."

"Sounds good to me."

"Thanks again," she tells me as we're getting ready to walk out the door. When I go to say something back, she stops me. "Seriously, I feel better than I have in years. I may not look it," she smiles as she points to her face, to the evidence of a night spent crying, "but I do feel better."

And with the sun shining, we walk along Fifth Avenue heading uptown to museum row. She has three mimosas to my two—I'm thinking she needs them—and after we finish exploring, we grab sandwiches from a deli and eat them sitting on the grass in Central Park. Grace looks wiped out when she lays back on the grass, and I follow her lead. And in that moment none of it matters: our sad pasts, the uncertainties that lie ahead. Looking up at the passing clouds with her hand in mine, I can't help but feel that this is the start of something good and real.

* * *

"Just another two hours in the car now," she jokes as we put our bags into the trunk after we finally locate my car in the airport's long-term parking lot. "Sure you're up for it?"

"It's no big deal," I tell her, even though my leg is sore from all the walking we've been doing these past few days. "You could stay at my place tonight, though. Then I'd drive you home tomorrow morning."

I'm glad to see she's on board with the idea. "Sure...I'd like to see you in your natural habitat."

"Good. I could go for a beer, some takeout, and watching tonight's game on the couch. Are you down for a mellow night?"

"Put a warm bath into that line-up and I'm definitely down."

I swat her butt as I hold the door open. "As long as I can get in there with you." And now I can't wait to get her back to my place.

This trip, as hard as it was in some ways, I'd still call it a win. To have Grace share something with me that she's kept hidden for years? In some strange way that fills me with pride. And the fact that she's come to know so much about what I've gone through with my injury puts me at ease. She's seen my residual limb in all its deformed glory, and watched as I hopped around the doctor's office when the tech took my prosthetic. I'm not self-conscious around her at all.

She looks around when we get to my place, making her way from the entryway to the living room and then the kitchen. "This puts my place to shame, Hanson."

"It's fairly new construction...All shiny and new. Yours has character."

She rolls her eyes. "Nice try."

"I can help you get some work done. I'm off until the end of July."

"How would that work if you did decide to go ahead with the surgery?" She takes a seat at the kitchen island and looks down at my leg. "The rehabilitation time—"

"I'd have to take a full semester off. There's no other way. So that's officially on the back burner."

"And your leg feels all right now?" I can tell by her face that she knows it doesn't. "We put a lot of miles in this week."

"I'm a runner, so I'm used to it, but every time you get a new leg it's an adjustment."

She winks at me and smiles as she gets up. "A good excuse for me to run that bath."

"I'm ordering our food now," I call out over the sound of running water. "There's a great Thai place that delivers but they take forever."

I pour us two glasses of wine and walk into the bathroom to see her lounging back with her eyes closed. Her hair is piled up on top of her head, showcasing her slender neck and her shoulders.

I realize in that moment that I was never attracted to Ava the way I am to Grace. No woman has ever made me feel so much.

"Solid move, bucking up for the oversized tub."

"It came with the house. I don't use it enough, but maybe now that you're in the picture…"

"I'd just like to go on record as saying that shower and tub sex are highly overrated."

"Come again?"

"Soaking is magnificent." She sits up and gestures for me to scoot in behind her once I've got my leg off. "And soaking with a hot guy is the absolute best." Resting back against me, she puts her wineglass on the ledge with mine and then guides my hands so that I'm touching her breasts. "But penetration in the tub, in a river or the ocean? No bueno. It's irritating."

"You've tested this theory out?"

She turns around, changing positions so that we're chest to chest, and my Lord, the feel of her wet skin on mine is as close as I'll ever get to heaven. "I'm certainly not a virgin," she tells me as she shifts her hips to press against my dick.

I run my hands down her back, cup her ass and give her a squeeze. "I've never gone deep sea diving with a girl, so I'll take your word for it."

"No shower sex?"

"Yes to the shower, no to the ocean, river or lake experience. And it's not like I was a saint or anything, but the opportunity just never came up."

"You didn't miss out on anything. Trust me."

Slipping one hand lower, I cup her between the legs and she lets out a sexy little whimper. "Sure it doesn't feel good?"

"Mmm...It's this, the lead up that feels good." She rolls her hips to get off on the contact. "But I prefer a bed or dry land for the missile launch."

"Fuck," I let out on a laugh. "The missile launch?"

"Yeah." She reaches down between us. "And this missile packs a punch, but there's plenty of time for fun and games later." She turns back around and rests against me, reaches for our glasses and hands one to me. "This is nice," she whispers after taking a sip of her wine.

"It's just what I needed." And I mean it. I've needed whatever this is. Intimacy, touch, comfort. I take another sip of my wine and slip my free arm underneath Grace's breasts, resting there.

I could fall in love with this girl.

# Chapter Twenty-Nine

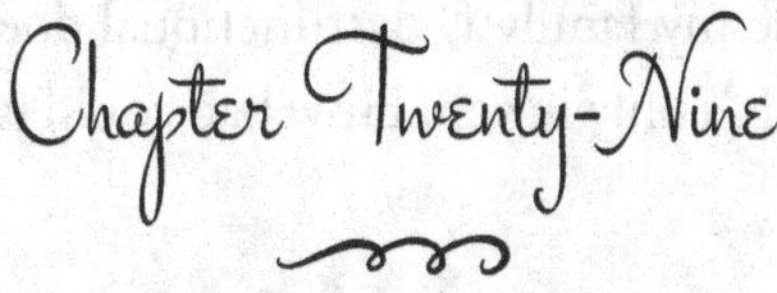

## GRACE

"I don't want to take you home."

"Can't say that I want to go, but I do need to check my mail, water my plants and," I look down at the wrinkled shirt that's doing double duty, "get some laundry done."

Last night was as perfect as it gets. Sweatpants and t-shirts, on the couch drinking wine and eating yummy noodles right out of the takeout containers. We huddled together watching the Pirates kick the Reds' butts, and then curled up together in bed. No sex. Too tired. But it didn't matter one bit. Maybe it was even better because we didn't.

"Ugh," he groans looking down at his phone. "My mother just left a message reminding me about lunch again." He looks over to me to gauge my reaction and I'm pretty sure I'm giving off a deer in the headlights look. "Too soon to meet the fam?" he asks, and when I nod, he says, "I thought so."

I'm thinking it's *way* too soon. Like, I could marry Owen and never feel the need to introduce him to my crazy assortment of parents and step-parents. I hardly even know the twins my father inherited when he married the young hottie who used to manage his radiology practice. But when Owen smiles at me, I can see that he's masking disappointment.

Just because my family is dysfunctional doesn't mean that every family is. It's only lunch. How bad could it be?

* * *

Awful.

It was seriously awful.

Imagine having a tooth pulled while undergoing a Brazilian wax for the first time with no prep. Yeah, if given the option I'd go for the wax-tooth pull combo without a second thought.

Sunday brunch is apparently a *thing* in the Hanson home. Owen's parents, the Honorable Maxwell Hanson and his bride of thirty-nine years, Marianne, are picture perfect. *My bride of thirty-nine years*—that's how she was introduced.

She also carries the title of hostess extraordinaire because the woman cooked an entire table full of delectable dishes single-handedly. My own mother would scoff at the effort it took to pull off a spread like that.

I should mention that while Owen's father bestowed maybe ten seconds of attention on me, his mother saw no such need. She said nothing when we were introduced. Nada. She was wide-eyed when we walked in the door holding hands, looking over her shoulder every two seconds to where a crowd was mingling on the back deck.

"Who's here?" Owen asked her.

She forced a smile. "Oh, just a few friends, Aunt Jane...The Palmers."

"Are you kidding me?" I don't even know if Owen realized

that he dropped my hand like a hot potato when he added, "Maybe you should have mentioned that in your message."

"Owen." She shook her head as if to tell him, a grown man, that he was behaving badly.

Palmer, I would soon come to find out, is Ava's last name, and the two families aren't just old friends, as Owen described them, but are more like extended family. The moms are best friends, the dads went to law school together, and Owen's two sisters think of Ava as a beloved big sis. But not, you know, in an Owen and Ava incest weird sorta way.

I did my best, I really did. I smiled when I was introduced, attempted small talk even though I felt like I had a stone lodged in my throat, and I'm pretty sure I managed to keep my very nervous hands from shaking.

But after choking down an extra spicy *virgin* bloody Mary —seriously, what's the point?—and a few nibbles of the yummy frittata I normally would have devoured, I wanted out.

Owen stayed by my side as his sisters fussed over him and made polite, forced chitchat with me, he ran interference when his aunt started asking intrusive questions about my background, and he held my hand when Ava's mother made a show of looking me over from head to toe.

Did I mention that brunch was a smart-casual affair, and I was dressed one hundred percent casual, complete with wrinkles? Me, the queen of the sundress? Well, today I was wearing unwashed jeans, my last pair of clean underwear, and a t-shirt that I managed to spill tomato juice on when I took my first sip of that crappy drink.

At one point poor Owen had to use the bathroom, and when he left it was an uncomfortable five minutes before I heard raised voices coming from the backyard. Owen's mother moved closer so that she could overhear, but that proved unnecessary. When Owen turned and started to walk back towards the house, everyone within a mile probably heard Ava shout after him, "I think I'm pregnant!"

With my heart beating out of my chest, I put my glass on the marble countertop—I really hope I left a permanent tomato juice stain on that bad boy—then walked out the door, grabbed my bags from Owen's car and headed down their street, my free hand trembling as I cued up the ride share app on my phone.

I didn't pick up when my phone rang a few minutes later and I didn't open his texts.

One long hour and seventy-five dollars later, I was back home.

Safe and sound and alone.

# Chapter Thirty

OWEN

I round on her, pointing my finger in her face. "You're not pregnant, so let's just cut the shit, ok?"

"How could you, Owen?"

"How could I what?"

"Bring some random girl *here*, home with you?"

"Grace isn't some random girl, and last I checked, this is *my* house."

I let out a weary breath, angry at myself for making this any harder on Ava than it has to be. I remind myself that she's not an evil person, and that even though she had it coming, I did hurt her when I broke it off.

Pinching the bridge of my nose, I make the effort to be civil. "I didn't mean to yell at you. I'm sorry." When she goes to plead her case, I shake my head to stop her. "I have to get back inside."

My plan is to whisk Grace the hell out of this shitshow and drive her back home. Figure I'll deal with my family later on.

But when I don't find her in the kitchen or the living room, and my mother meets me at the front door saying, "I think your friend left," I unleash on her.

"You were rude. I'm ashamed of you, of dad, and of you two little bitches."

My mother gasps and then looks around to see if anyone else heard that, while my sisters stand there shocked. I've never spoken to anyone in my family like this before. Up until today they've never given me reason to.

"I'm serious. If you did anything to screw this up for me, any one of you," I add, looking directly at my two sisters, "I will never forgive you."

I'm hoping against hope that she's waiting for me out in the car, even though I know in my gut that she's long gone. I drive down the street, searching the side streets for her with no luck, and then pull over to call her phone. I'm not surprised when it goes straight to voicemail.

She only answers when I text: *Just let me know that you're ok*.

And her response a full hour later leaves no doubt as to how fucked I am.

*I'm fine. Just got home. Please DO NOT come here.*

I want to put my foot on the gas and speed right to her, but something tells me to turn the other way and head back to my place. I get the feeling that if I don't respect her wishes, I'll lose her.

* * *

I hop up, not bothering with my leg, and hop over to my front door when I hear someone knocking a few hours later. I leave the door open and turn away disappointed when I see that it's just my mother and my two sisters wearing apologetic smiles and carrying plates of food.

"We're sorry, O," my youngest sister Willa starts off.

"Truly, Hon," my mother adds, "If I knew you were bringing a friend home I would have told you Ava was going to be there." When I bark out a laugh she rushes to add, "I never would have invited the Palmers over."

"It would have been pretty easy to pass that information along. And even if I wasn't bringing someone home, why were you trying to get me alone in a room with Ava and her family? Are you all playing matchmaker or something?"

"But why don't you like Ava?" my sister Nan whines. "She's perfect for you!"

"She's not," I tell all of them as I take the foil off one of the plates and dig into my mother's noodle pudding. "I'm not getting back together with Ava so you'd better get over it."

"Grace seemed very nice," my mother offers up cautiously.

"And she's prettier than Ava."

"Willa, that's a crappy thing to say!"

"Shut up, Nan. You were laughing behind Grace's back before, cracking on her clothes."

"Girls!" They both stop, and even I turn to look because my mother sounds downright apocalyptic right now. "Go out to the car and wait for me." When they don't hop to it, she all but screams, "Now!"

She comes over to join me at the island and then sighs when I go on ignoring her. "You never told me why the two of you broke up. I never understood it."

"I'm thirty-five. You're not entitled to updates on my love life and you don't have to understand."

"Ava just seems so crushed over it."

"She'll survive. And what she said back at the house?" I

look up from my plate. "Sorry, but you're not about to be a grandma."

"Oh, Owen." She shakes her head. "Are you sure she's not in trouble?"

I can't help but roll my eyes. "I'm sure. And that little performance? Typical Ava. I know you think Ava's a saint, but she's not. She's manipulative, and for the life of me, I don't know what drove me to get involved with her in the first place. I was never really into her in high school, and I—"

"But life has changed since then...Life has changed for you."

I get up, hop over to the sink and slam the dish in with force, not giving a damn if it breaks. Making my way over to the couch where I left my leg, I tell her, "I get it. You still see me as a cripple. Like I should be grateful that Ava or any other woman would want to be with me."

"I do not!"

"You do." I'm boiling with rage, madder still when I acknowledge that the feeling is fueled by a deep-seated shame that I haven't confessed to in years. "You worry about me all the fucking time. Look around," I gesture to nothing in partic-ular, "I have a home, a good career, friends...I don't deserve to be pitied." When she goes to speak, I stop her. "Ava might come off as well-meaning, but she's the same. I think in her warped mind she believed moving in with me was some act of benevolence on her part or something...Like she was going to be my very own Florence Nightingale."

"Isn't it possible that she simply cares about you?"

"She lied about needing a place to stay for a few months, played on my sympathy. And I hate to break it to you, but her ex-husband isn't the monster she's made him out to be. Ava cheated on *him*. That's why he kicked her out. So now she's on the hunt for a new husband who can provide her with the life-style she's become accustomed to. She saw me as an easy mark."

"I've known Ava for most of her life. I can't believe—"

"I'm not asking you to believe me, and I'm not asking you to sever ties with Ava or the Palmers. I'm just *telling* you that if you want me in your life, you need to respect me and the choices I make."

Her voice is barely above a whisper when she says, "I think it's best that I go now."

*Don't let the door hit your ass on the way out.* Those words are on the tip of my tongue, but I hold back. What she did today was wrong, plain and simple, but both of them, my mother and my father, have made sacrifices for me and they've been in my corner since the day I was born.

"Owen." I turn to see her standing in the doorway looking defeated. "Believe me when I say that I never meant to make you feel that way. I'm proud of you and I always have been. I hope you know that."

# Part Three

## RIGHT WHERE YOU LEFT ME

# Chapter Thirty-One

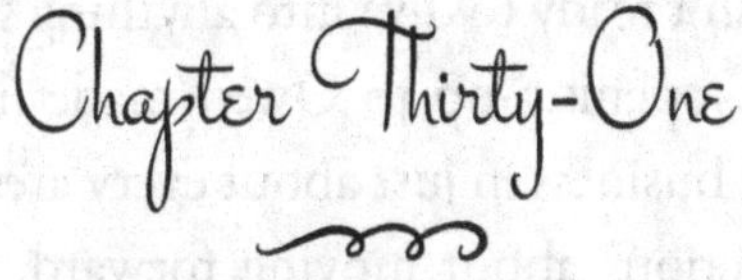

GRACE

"Do you think we can get this done before school starts up? I'm due back in less than two weeks."

Garth surveys the kitchen, which is now gutted down to the studs. "Flooring is done. Sheetrock and painting won't take too long. Cabinets and countertops are scheduled to go in on Wednesday." He shrugs. "As long as the electrician and the plumber show up and finish on time, I don't see why not."

"That's what I wanted to hear."

The kitchen is last on the list of home improvement projects I need to tackle. With a whole lotta help from Garth, my non-licensed, quasi general contractor, I've painted the exterior of the house, hung new shutters, replaced the front door, removed every scrap of flowered wallpaper from the bedrooms, and changed out all the light fixtures. The walls are now painted in coastal grays and pale blues, and once the dust settles from the kitchen remodel, I'll be able to move my furniture out of storage and back into *my* house. I'm trying not to call it Aunt Viv's house but it's still hard.

It's been a summer.

After that God awful meet-the-parents fiasco, I let Owen know that I wasn't ready to dive into anything serious.

If anything, opening up to Owen made me realize that I have unfinished business in just about every area of my life, and if I was truly serious about moving forward, I needed to do some soul searching in terms of my past.

I've come to dub this: *Operation Coming Clean*, and my first mission? A visit to my brother and his wife out in San Diego. Figured I'd start off easy, and a long weekend at their sunny beachside home was just what the doctor ordered. The sun, the surf, and the love of family made spilling my truth and my tears less painful than I expected. And who knew? It gets easier every time you do it.

Doctor Clare Dawson will never be the Marmee to my Jo March, but I'm building a relationship with my mother now and that's a good thing.

Both my mother and my father had questions—lots of them—and I knew they both felt bad about not seeing the signs or even suspecting something was wrong with me back then. They weren't the perfect parents, they fell short in many ways, but for that I'll never blame them. I was as secretive as a CIA operative in my formative years, so there's no way they could have known, even if they *were* paying attention.

*Can you contact her parents? Do you know where she lives? When will she legally be able to seek you out? What is her name?* I answered as best as I could. *I know her parents' first names and I know they were living in New Jersey when the adoption was finalized. I think she can seek me out when she's eighteen but I'm not sure. No, I don't know her name.* And I don't tell them that I call her Birdie in the quiet of my own mind. *Who is the father?* I tell them who Damien *was*, and I tell them that he's gone. It all hurts, but that's the part that physically pains me deep when I say the words out loud.

Damien.

Every time I started to clean out Aunt Viv's house, some force would draw me to the shelves and have me reaching up for that book where the pictures were stashed. I'd sit back on the couch, stare at them and get lost in the past.

But now those pictures are framed. I took them to a professional when I was in Philly visiting my mother, and now they're matted, airtight and framed in a way that will stand up to the test of time. They're in a box, safe in the bedroom closet. I'll hang them someday, but not now.

In late July I reached out to Frannie and Reese, and we set up a girl's weekend down at Frannie's beach house in Nags Head. It was a wine-soaked, emotional get together filled with mostly laughter, but some tears. Frannie couldn't get over the fact that they never realized I was pregnant, even though I was more than six months along by the time school broke for summer.

Reese cracked, "That only happens with the first pregnancy. You pop immediately the second, third and fourth time."

"I can't wait to pop," Frannie said, smiling down at her belly.

And I'll admit, while it was hard to hear about Reese's children and the excitement over Frannie's first pregnancy after struggling to conceive for so long, I was happy for them, and happy to have them back in my life again.

I did trip and fall once while traveling down the road to redemption, and nothing could have prepared me for it.

The last time I saw Gianna Oliveri was sometime in January, a couple of months after Damien was deployed.

I'd written three or four letters to every one Damien sent back, and at that point I hadn't heard a word from him in over a month. My last three letters came off as increasingly frantic, and in my very last letter I told him I was pregnant, with the due date written in angry block letters.

Crickets.

I still wasn't desperate enough to go knocking on her door or her brother Eli's. I was too proud. But when I practically ran smack right into her on campus one day, I broke down and asked her in the most roundabout way possible if she had any news.

But the girl was like a shark getting her first taste of blood in the water. She cocked her head to the side, surprised and downright gleeful. "You haven't heard from him?"

"I have," I hedged. "Just not in the past two weeks."

Make that six weeks.

"Um, yeah, he emails us all the time. I just got one last night. He received the care package I sent, so he was just reaching out to say thank you." She laughed. "Oh, and he was telling me about some drama between the new recruits and how one of them..."

I can only imagine that I looked close to tears when she trailed off mid-sentence.

"Hey," she looked down at her phone, letting me know that I was wasting time she could be spending with other, more interesting people, "I'm sure you'll hear from him soon enough." She started to walk but then stopped and turned to look over her shoulder. "Grace?" She gave me a quick once over before landing her parting shot. "You don't look so good. Maybe you need to get some rest...or hit the gym."

I wanted to slap her face. And his.

He was sending emails to *her*? Eli I could understand. Maybe even Eli's parents. But he didn't even ask for *my* email address. Nope, I was reduced to second-rate snail mail, and apparently Damien was afflicted with a bad case of writer's cramp.

Walking away, I remember beating myself up over not sending him care packages. The thought never crossed my mind. I pictured him opening a box filled with his favorite snacks, lip balm, dry socks, and other things any moron would instinctively know that a soldier needed while stranded out in the middle of the desert. She probably tucked a note inside, too. Maybe even a picture with her smiling and looking her best.

I resigned myself to the fact that Damien wasn't the man I thought he was. He was in love when he wanted to fuck, but not so in love with the consequences of fucking.

Heartbroken and angry, I wasn't the least bit hungry, but forced myself to nourish the life growing inside of me. All I wanted to do was sleep, but I got up every morning and dragged myself to class. I didn't have a game plan, I was just going through the motions.

Another month passed before I heard that Eli had taken his own life. Frannie, a fellow nursing major, told me Gianna hadn't been to class in weeks, and then heard the grim news from a professor who was starting a collection for the scholarship fund the family had set up in his name. Frannie was the one who sat me down and told me that Damien was killed in the line of duty, and that Eli had taken his own life soon after.

I never reached out to Gianna. I was walking through life like a zombie at that point, overwhelmed by a combination of guilt, grief and fear. I just kept going, putting one foot after the other.

So after I checked into a hotel in Durham last month and dialed her number, I was more than just a little bit nervous. I had no idea how this was going to go.

She was quiet for a moment and then whispered my name when I told her who was calling. "Grace?"

"Yes, Grace Dawson. How are you, Gianna?"

"Why are you calling?"

*Still the same old sweetheart I remember.*

"I'm calling because I'm in town, and I wanted to know if you had any information about where Damien is buried. He didn't have any family, and I haven't been able to get information from the government because I'm not listed as kin. I know how close he was to your family so I was hoping you could help me out."

"You want to visit his grave?"

"I do. And Gianna, I should have reached out to you a long time ago. I was so sorry to hear about Eli."

She cleared her throat and then sighed. "Damien is buried next to him in our family plot."

Trembling, I couldn't keep the emotion from my voice. "That's good. He would have wanted that. He loved Eli like a brother."

She rattled off the name of the cemetery and some basic directions to lead me to the spot. Her goodbye was quick and curt. I ended the call shaking my head. After all these years the girl still intimidated me.

The next day I was up bright and early.

And so was Gianna.

I was crouched down, running my fingers over the words engraved on his headstone: *Beloved Son, Devoted Friend.*

"Father," I whispered as I ran my fingers over the empty space where that word should be.

"I knew you were pregnant." I'm not the least bit startled or surprised by the interruption. "I saw you one day when I was out running errands with my mother that summer. You were huge."

Standing up, I looked over my shoulder to see her chewing gum and staring off into the distance. Never in a million years would I expect Gianna to go all warm and fuzzy on me. No, even an olive branch would be delivered with a side of snark.

She moved to stand beside me, leaving a few feet of space.

"I thought Damien would be buried in Arlington."

"He could have been. Eli too, but my parents wanted them both close by. Damien had my parents listed as his next of kin."

I debated over whether or not I even wanted to engage this girl, but then just went ahead and spewed my ugly truth. "I hated you for a long time. I mean, I felt terrible when I heard about Eli, but I still hated you for having some kind of hold over Damien."

"There was nothing there, and not for lack of trying on my part. Believe me, I *tried* to steal him away from you." We shared a sad laugh, the both of us looking down at the stone. "And I hated *you* because Damien loved you...Only you. I wanted to know what the hell you had that I didn't. I mean, I was—"

"You were prettier."

"Lot of good that did me." She glanced my way but still didn't make eye contact. "And you were gorgeous, Grace...You still are, you bitch. He looked at you like you were a juicy steak and a hot fudge sundae all rolled into one. It's like you had some voodoo spell cast over him."

"That day on campus when I stopped you...Do you remember that? When you told me Damien was writing to you?" I looked over to see her biting her lip and nodding. "I thought he'd used me, played me for a fool or something."

"I was lying."

"I know that now."

"I wanted to hurt you."

"You did, but I'm not angry about it anymore. I haven't been for a long time."

"What did you do? I missed two semesters after Eli died, but when I came back to campus you were a senior. I was commuting from home so I was totally out of the scene, but I saw you once or twice. You were never pushing a baby carriage."

"I gave her up for adoption right after I gave birth."

"I figured that." Gianna cleared her throat before telling me, "He would have come back for you, you know. And he would have made a great father." Wiping at her eyes, she gave my hand one gentle squeeze and then turned to leave. "Take care of yourself, Grace."

I knelt down again and ran one finger over the grooves and corners of his name, letter by letter.

"I know, Damien. I know you would have come back to me."

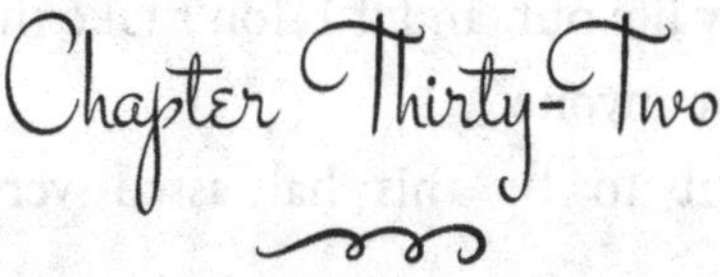

# Chapter Thirty-Two

GRACE

"I can't make it this Friday."

"Come on, he won't even be there." Skylar's got one hand over her heart. "I swear."

The girl has ambushed me, tagging along when Sienna drove over to pick up Garth.

We're in the home stretch now, and he's been giving me every day off and coming over most evenings after his shift at the hardware store, too. I pay him well, but I still feel like he's gone above and beyond for me. He hires all the day workers, and he's hooked me up with a great carpenter, an electrician and a plumber.

Right now we're picking out the kitchen faucet from a plumbing catalogue, and I need to make a choice on the cabinet hardware before Garth leaves, too. The clock is ticking, and Skylar is being a pain in my ass right now.

I've kept my distance.

We've texted a few times, me and Owen, but I've purposefully kept it surface level and light. He knows where I stand and he's respected my need for time and space.

I'm missing out on something that has the potential to be great, but I also know deep down that I am the only one who can straighten my life out, and if I don't take the time to do it I won't be good for anyone.

I don't want to be this half-assed version of myself anymore.

And Owen has some unfinished business, too.

Walking into his parents' house that day was a nightmare. I felt like an unwanted guest. Nope, scratch that—I *was* an unwanted guest. And while he never really told me the background story on his relationship with Ava, it was clear that they had a past that was deep-rooted in family.

When she screamed, *I'm pregnant,* for the world to hear? That wasn't even the final straw. Her declaration reeked of desperation, and I figured, just like Owen, that it was nonsense. No, it's what he said to Ava right after. I was frozen in place and you could have hard a pin drop at that point. So when he told her that he was sorry and that he shouldn't have yelled at her, I could hear the regret and the tenderness in his voice. He cared about her.

I was someone's second-best a long, long time ago, and I'll never go down that road again. And even though Owen did everything short of swearing on the bible when he told me over and over again that I was wrong and that he didn't have any romantic feelings for her, I didn't want to hear it.

I do have feelings for Owen, strong feelings, but I love myself more.

"He asks about you, Grace."

I circle my choices in the brochure, ignoring Skylar, and

then confirm the number and size of the drawer pulls and cabinet handles that we need.

When I turn back to face her, she's waiting on me with her arms crossed in front of her chest.

"How is Owen doing?"

"Good, I guess. I mean, he looks great. He just did a triathlon up in Nantucket with Leo and Max."

"Wow."

"He trains a lot. Leo said he's looking to do more competitive-length races this fall."

"That's great."

She throws her head back and fists her hands at her sides. "Aren't you going to ask me if he's seeing anyone else?"

Just the mention of Owen seeing another woman has me conjuring up crazy images. First it's him and Ava sloshing around in his big giant bathtub the way we did, then it's some hot triathlete girl and Owen crossing the finish line together hand in hand.

Skylar snaps her fingers in front of my face until I answer, "Nope, I don't want to know."

Then she crosses her arms over her chest and looks at me in a way that's borderline nasty. "I don't understand what you're doing. You're pushing a kind, good-hearted man away."

"A hot man, too. Don't leave that out," Sienna adds with a head nod.

"You two don't understand."

"Then enlighten us."

I look between the both of them, wondering if they'll judge me. For the most part, I've made peace with my past, but there's still that nagging, reproachful voice telling me that I did the wrong thing, that I was weak and cowardly to do what I did. But after a deep breath and a quick silent pep talk, I sit down on the stoop and they join me.

"Remember when we were talking about Charlotte Mason at your house a few months ago?"

"Yes," they say in unison, nodding their heads in tandem.

"That was hard for me. See, I knew Charlotte was pregnant back then...I mean, I suspected it. And I was trying to help when I told her about getting pregnant back when *I* was in college. It just struck me that I'd told a kid, one of my students, but I'd never shared that secret with anyone else before. Not my parents, not Jack, not anyone."

They both close in on me for a group hug, still holding me tight when I tell them the basics about Damien and about giving our daughter up for adoption. They both start to cry when I tell them he died before she was born.

And their reaction has been like all the rest. No one has made me feel ashamed, no one has chastised me. Every single time I've come clean, people only want to comfort me. Time and time again, I've come to realize that secrets and lies are nothing but a prison we build around ourselves.

"Do you understand now, Sky? I know Owen is a great guy, but I need this time to myself. I need to get my own house in order."

I don't tell them that Owen reminds me of Damien. I don't tell them that I could feel myself falling for Owen after just one week, fast and hard the same way I fell for Damien.

I do go down to the river after they leave, though. Just like always, I stand on the bank looking down into the slow and steady stream of water and listen for that whisper in the breeze. And just like always, I tell Damien everything.

# Chapter Thirty-Three

OWEN

Looking on from the outside, my life looks productive. My days are filled. I work out in the mornings, plan my fall curriculum in the afternoons, and I make plans to fill up at least three or four nights out of my week.

I enjoy training and I do enjoy my job, but I'm conscious of the effort I'm making to keep busy. Grace hasn't reached out to me in weeks, and she's made it clear that she wants time and space—from me.

I didn't imagine it. I know she was developing feelings for me. And while I know that she's going through a lot right now, I still don't understand why she wants to go through it all alone.

I pick my phone up again, looking for missed calls or a message from her. I'm over at Sky and Leo's for some end of summer barbecue, and I'm surrounded by happy couples and single women I have no interest in meeting. Honestly, I only came on the off chance that she'd be here.

Max asks Skylar, "How's your friend, Grace?"

She glances my way when she says, "She's good. I just saw her last week. Garth is working on her kitchen and it's almost finished, so she's up to her ears in the remodel."

"Leo told me she broke off her engagement to that guy."

"She did." Sky pauses then adds, "But she's seeing someone new." She turns to me and winks on the sly. "She seems happy."

Max is barely listening at this point. He tosses out, "That's good," as he moves towards a small group of Skylar's teaching buddies clustered over by the pool.

Skylar flops into a chair opposite me. "Last thing I want is Max hitting on any of my friends."

I look to where he's schmoozing a few ladies at the moment. "Too late."

"I meant my close friends. And what I said was a crock...You know that, right?"

"The part about her seeing someone, or about being happy?"

"She's not seeing anyone. I can't really speak to the happiness part."

I look down and nod. "I hope she's happy."

Skylar smacks her head. "Ugh! She says the same thing about you! When your name comes up she looks like she's been kicked in the gut, but then she smiles and tosses out that exact lame line. Do you *really* hope Grace is happy without you?"

"She knows where I stand. I can't force her to want to be with me."

"*Does* she know where you stand? Are you sure? If I were in her shoes and you just gave up when I told you to go, I don't know...I'd think maybe I wasn't all that important to you."

"You don't know—"

"Everything she's been dealing with? I do. She told me. And I know she confided in you, too. Do you really think she wants to be alone in all this?"

I don't answer because I really don't have a clue.

Skylar reaches over and puts a hand on my shoulder. "No pain, no gain. Isn't that what you guys always say? Go to her, Owen. Worst thing that can happen is she turns you away and you're no worse off than you are now. But stop wasting time."

* * *

I spend the next few weeks doing just that, wasting time. I visit one of my old naval academy buddies at his beach house in Jersey, do another sprint triathlon with my sister Willa over Labor Day weekend, and then I'm back into my fall routine of teaching and work-related obligations. But I think about her every damn day.

That night we spent at her house, our trip to New York—I replay every kiss, touch, and the words spoken over and over in my mind. Being with Grace was good in every way. In bed, out of bed, talking to her and just holding her close were the best times I've ever had with a woman.

I don't want to close the book on what we were just starting. And this hurts, so fucking bad.

People mean well but they don't understand. My family walks on eggshells around me, and my mother gingerly asking if I might want to bring Grace over for dinner one night gets her nothing but a growl. Friends who think they're doing me a favor by introducing me to their sisters, single friends or coworkers make me want to ram my head into the nearest wall.

I want her.

No one else.

# Chapter Thirty-Four

## GRACE

This little shindig is for my friends and for the people who helped me accomplish this labor of love, it's not for me.

I pick a few stray weeds from the flower beds, pleased when I take a step back and take it all in. The house came out better than I ever could have hoped for.

It's Nantucket meets Western Pennsylvania, if that's even a thing.

The exterior siding is painted a cobblestone gray, with new windows, shutters and window boxes all trimmed in white. I take another moment to admire the navy blue craftsman-style door, and I'm loving how the big full hydrangeas are blooming purple against this beautiful new home.

I've tried to call it home, *my home*, but those words are like a pair of shoes that are my size but still don't fit.

But it's no matter. Every new home deserves a housewarming, a before and after big reveal, a coming out party.

Walking around to the back, I straighten the cushions on

the new patio furniture, plug the string lights in, and cue up a playlist for the speakers. Lately I find myself veering towards somber songs about lost loves. Story of my life, I suppose.

This one is about a boy who still pines for a girl after breaking her heart back when they were seventeen. Mistakes and missed opportunities.

I make a mental note to play more upbeat tunes during the party, but as the song plays out it's final chorus with the lyrics repeating *I miss you*, I can't help but think of Owen.

He's pretty much always on my mind. He did what I asked, gave me time and gave me space. I haven't had so much as a text from him in over a month and it serves me right.

What did I expect? That a kind-hearted, good-looking man like him would wait around until I got my act together? That he wouldn't have women beating a path to his door? He works on a college campus. I'm sure he's got a whole line of graduate assistants looking to scoop him up like Jack's little protégé did.

No, I can't go there now.

I walk inside, pour myself a glass of wine and then come back to enjoy the warm September air as I write out a shopping list for tomorrow.

I hear a car pull into the driveway and raise up a silent prayer that one of my guests didn't get the date wrong. My money is on Garth.

Letting out a frustrated breath, I drag myself out of my comfy chair to see who's guilty of crashing a day early. But I only make it two steps before he turns the corner and stops to stand before me.

And I know these past few months have changed me because I'm no longer able to paste on that convincing smile. I'm basically incapable of faking it nowadays.

So when Owen pulls a small bouquet of the most perfect

orange roses out from behind his back, I can't help but cry when I try to speak.

"Hey, shh, don't cry. I'm sorry for just dropping in like this."

I shake my head so that he knows I'm not upset, so he knows that I want him here.

"I—I want you here, Owen."

He lets out a breath. "Thank God. I thought you were just about to send me packing."

I wipe at my watery eyes, embarrassed. "I'm such a disaster. It's just that I was sitting here thinking about you and it's like, my God, here you are."

"I really shouldn't have shown up without calling first, but I had to see you."

He puts the flowers down and waits until I look him in the eye. "Grace, I have to know if I have a shot here. I don't want to wait forever." He adds quietly, "I won't."

"If you'll have me, then I'd say you have more than a shot."

He nods, looking down to the ground. "You know how hard it was staying away these past few months?"

"I'd say I'm sorry, but I wasn't lying when I told you I needed time."

"No, I get that, I do, but every day we were apart just felt empty."

He's the one who's taken all the risks so far, so I move closer and take his hands in mine. "I don't need any more time. I know what I want."

"I kept telling myself I was crazy, you know? Kept telling myself that I hardly know you, but that's not how it feels."

And I understand because I feel the same way. "I think you know me better than anyone, Owen."

He shakes his head. "I don't, but I want to."

"Come." I gesture for him to follow when I walk inside.

"It looks so different in here."

"Needing time wasn't about getting this house sorted, but I think this place was a metaphor for my life. I've been running but going nowhere. I've been stuck for years. Does that make sense?"

"Yeah, it does."

He walks into the living room, checks it out and then looks back to me. "Go ahead," I tell him. "We did every room."

"Who helped you?" he asks as he inspects the molding around the bedroom windows. "The work is good."

"Garth will be pleased to hear that. He did the bulk of it with the help of a few skilled workmen."

Smiling at me, he says, "This is definitely more *you*. Especially now that the creepy Hummel figurine collection is gone. I can picture you in this place."

"Don't laugh, those Hummels went for big bucks on some online auction site."

He smiles and then goes to walk back into the living room. "Owen, wait." I lift the box from the closet and rest it on the bed. "I want to show you something."

And I hope I'm not making a big mistake when I take one of the pictures out from its bubble wrap, but if I'm on a mission to be an open book then I can't go on hiding things between the pages.

"I framed these so I'll have something to show...her. If she ever comes looking for me and wants," I pause to take a breath, "to know about him."

He takes the frame from my hands and studies the picture. He keeps looking, a soft smile forming on his face as he holds it up closer to get a better look. "Look how beautiful you were." He raises his eyes to mine. "You still are, Grace, but I love how you look in this shot." He looks back down. "And he was crazy about you. It's written all over his face."

"I went to visit his gravesite."

"Where is Damien buried?"

And just that, Owen's willingness to acknowledge Damien and speak his name—I'm grateful for it. It speaks to what I've always known about Owen: he's a strong man, self-possessed and unafraid, and he's also a good person.

"Down in North Carolina. Not far from where I went to school. He's buried next to a close friend, a fellow Marine who took his own life after he came back."

He nods. "That life takes its toll on some men. Damien?"

"No, he was killed in the line of duty."

I take the picture, wrap it and box it back up before I return them to the closet.

"You're not going to hang them?"

"No, not here." I answer the question in his eyes, "This isn't where I'm meant to be. I'm going to finish out the school year because I'm committed to my students, but I'm resigning come June."

He looks concerned when he asks, "Are you leaving?"

I raise my shoulders and smile. "I don't know. And I'm kind of all right with not knowing."

He wraps me up and kisses the top of my head before whispering, "We'll figure it out."

"Yeah," I melt into the hug, so glad to be back in his arms, "we will."

# Chapter Thirty-Five

GRACE

"I'm glad you were able to get a babysitter."

"Grandy's always up for some one-on-one time with James."

"She never turns us down," Sienna says, smiling at Garth. "I tease him about his mom, but I swear, I don't know what we'd do without her."

"Here, Sienna, have a seat," Owen says as he leads her to the pillowy-soft chaise I bought for the living room.

"I'm pregnant, people, not dying," she says on a laugh.

He shakes his head to tell her he's not having it. "You're pregnant with number three though, so take a load off."

I've come to realize that you really can be happy and sad at the same time. Taking in Owen's expression, it's so clear that he'd love a child of his own one day—and I'm thinking one day in the not so far off future. He knows it's a tender subject, so he hasn't come out and asked me point blank, but the way he fusses over Olivia, and the way he looks whenever we're at

255

Leo's house and there's a mess of kids over, it's written all over his face. I don't blame him. He's going to make a great father, same way Damien was made to play that role.

Most people break the year up at January and June, but not me. It's like the year starts on August 12th and the halfway mark is February 12th. Her birthday is the never far off my radar. So as I helped to decorate the gym for the last high school Valentine's Day dance I'll ever chaperone at my school, the red hearts signified another milestone. She's fifteen and a half now, soon to be sweet sixteen.

Garth follows me into the kitchen. "Is there anything wrong? When you said you had to talk to me about something important, I was worried I'd screwed up somewhere."

"Nothing is wrong."

"You'd tell me, right?" he asks as he takes the pitcher from my hand, helping to lighten my load as I take a plate of stuffed mushrooms back into the living room. "If you don't like how something came out, or if the sinks aren't draining or whatever, I hope you'd tell me."

"Relax. I absolutely love what you did here and everything works just fine."

Owen takes over, as it's clear I haven't convinced him. "Did you ever think about working towards a contractor's license? You're a natural at it, Garth."

"That's what I've been telling him!" Sienna sits up straight and points at her husband, "Haven't I been saying that, honey?"

"You have," he looks at her, smiling with so much affection, "but I just figured you were blowing smoke up my butt."

"We wanted to have you over to discuss something entirely different."

Owen continues, "It *is* about the house, but not about the

work." Fixing Garth with a look and nodding, he adds, "You did a great job here."

And I can see that coming from Owen, another man, an *older* man, the compliment means a great deal to Garth.

"So?" Sienna asks, "What's up?"

I've rehearsed this proposition a few dozen times, knowing they're going to say no as a reflex, but I have to convince them. The idea first came to me when we were in the middle of the renovations last summer, but over the course of the past several months I've come to see this as the best possible outcome for all of us.

The night they invited us over for the holidays completely sealed the deal.

* * *

The Perillo girls love to cook, and they're very good at it, but baking is Sienna's passion. Therefore, Christmas is Sienna's time to shine. The girl cannot stop. I swear that I put on five pounds between Thanksgiving and New Year's Day thanks to her. Peanut butter kiss cookies, candy cane bark, and her newest, a pinwheel concoction that tastes like a cinnamon roll, had me wearing leggings under my sweaters every day of winter break, as the top button on my jeans was not happening.

The weekend before Christmas, they invited us over for a cookie swap dinner party, along with Skylar, Leo and Olivia. Sienna served up a four-course dinner that was Michelin-star worthy, in my opinion, and Garth kept our glasses full all night.

I was helping her clear plates when I stopped in my tracks to look around their immaculate, shoebox-sized kitchen. I'd really call it a kitchen nook, as the cooking and dining areas were one in the same. How, I wondered, did she manage to put a meal like this together?

Joining the others in the living room, I took notice of the small tabletop tree, lit up and decorated with homespun ornaments, and of the festive knickknacks that fought for real estate on just about every surface. Neat as a pin, but bursting at the seams is how I'd describe the decor.

I watched Sienna and Garth navigate an obstacle course every time one of them made a trip to get someone another drink, or to attend to one of the children. James, at just a few months shy of his second birthday, was always on the move, and Rose, still tiny at just two months old, rested in a car seat on the floor, which Olivia tripped over several times.

No one but me seemed to notice. Everyone else was hopped up and happily tipsy, either from the multitude of sugary deserts or from Garth's holiday peppermint cosmopolitans, which after three of them, Skylar stood up and said, "From this day forward I decree that this delicious cocktail will be called Sex in the Boonies."

Leo poured her a water soon after.

I couldn't help but compare their home to mine. There was nothing wrong with where they lived, it was beautifully maintained, and more importantly, the place radiated love and warmth, but I was one person inhabiting a two-bedroom house with a spacious living room, a nice-sized kitchen and two full bathrooms.

"What's up?" Skylar nudged my knee, breaking me out of my thoughts. "Are you all right?"

"Yeah, fine," I answered, pasting on a smile. "I was just thinking that Sienna should have her own show on one of those cooking channels."

"She's amazing," Skylar agreed, but I could see in her eyes

that she was thinking along the same lines as me: *It's amazing what she can accomplish given that she has so little.*

We stayed up a few hours after the kids passed out, and since Sienna just announced she was pregnant again, she drove the four of us back to my house. Olivia had negotiated a sleepover, but it was just more practical for Leo and Sky to take the guest bedroom at my place. We didn't discuss it beforehand, but really, there was nowhere for them to stay in the trailer.

"Don't be silly, I have an air mattress all ready to go," Sienna answered when I suggested they crash with us. I felt bad about it the next morning, thinking back on her expression, a mixture of disappointment and acceptance.

"Coffee," Sky whispered, joining me in the kitchen.

"Feeling all right?" I teased.

"I think those drinks were pure booze with a candy cane crushed in it."

"*Those* drinks? Um, Queen Skylar, you *decreed* they be called Sex in the Boonies from this day forward."

Leo joined us then, already showered and looking fresh as a daisy. "Here ye, here ye, henceforth and forever more...Don't forget that part."

"Ugh...Sex in the what?"

"Boonies," he answered, tussling her hair. "Maybe you could pitch a reality show with that title."

"Good one," she muttered, lowering her head to rest on the table. "Never. Drinking. Again."

"Sienna packed up some lemon poundcake for our breakfast," I said, setting the plate on the table.

"She's a trip." Leo then proceeded to moan the moment he took a bite. "Man, this is heavenly."

And my friend wasn't hurting that badly, as she was able to

waggle her eyes in response to his reaction. "I can make that for you at home later on."

"Promises, promises. I predict an afternoon on the couch watching sappy Christmas romance movies while nursing that hangover."

"That sounds good, too."

Looking to me, Leo added, "She's got Olivia hooked on them now. My daughter thinks she's going to marry a lumberjack who runs a Christmas tree farm."

"And she'll be the high-powered, hard-nosed business mogul who's looking to buy the land out from under him to build a shopping mall, correct?"

"Yep."

"I'm curious..." Stalling for a moment, I questioned whether or not I should even get into it, knowing I might be overstepping, and not really knowing if Skylar would take offense on her sister's behalf. "Do the two of them own their place or rent?"

Meanwhile, I knew damn well they were renting.

"They rent it. Sienna said they get a good price because the owner is the same man who's been renting to Garth's mother for years." Skylar took a sip of her coffee, then another, all the while looking out the window. It was another full minute before she said, "It's tiny, isn't it?"

"Garth's a big guy, but I guess he's used to it, having grown up in something so similar. I hit my head on the top of the bathroom doorframe twice last night," Leo said as he rubbed at a spot on his forehead.

"I just wonder if what they're paying now would be comparable to renting this place."

Skylar no longer had any trace of a hangover. "You're moving in with Owen?"

I gestured for her to shush. "We've talked about it—"

"And you're there practically *all* the time as it is now," she finished for me.

"No I'm not, Sky. I still have a job."

Leo said, "You've mentioned moving on, though."

I nodded, "Oh, I'm set on resigning at the end of this term. I don't know where I'm going to teach, or if I'm even going to teach come September, but I'm making a change. I was thinking of taking some time off to figure it out, at least a semester. And if I'm doing that, I probably should do something with the house. Seems a shame for it to just sit here empty, right?"

# Chapter Thirty-Six

GRACE

Skylar and Leo have Fridays penciled in for date night, and they have Meatless Mondays on the dinner schedule every week—no exceptions. Our other friends with children have similar routines: the local diner after Sunday Mass, board game night, family movie night, etc.

The nice thing about being a new couple with no kids in the mix? Your routines can be nonexistent, or they can be spicier.

Every Friday afternoon I tidy up my classroom, wash out the vase I use for the fresh flowers that have started to wilt, and fill in my day planner so that I feel organized and ready to go when I come in on Monday morning. I go home to water the plants and clean out my fridge, and then I hit the road.

Our Friday night routine consists of my favorite Thai take out, which is best eaten from containers that Owen and I pass back and forth while sitting on the couch, a bottle of our favorite pinot noir, and a bubble bath. That's the pregame, anyway.

"Man, I'm so full," Owen says as he lowers himself in behind me.

Settling back against him, I murmur, "This right here is the best part of my week."

Lifting his hips and nudging me from behind, he teases, "The bath is the best part? Maybe I have to up my game."

"Your game is solid, trust me," I assure him as I secure his free hand and slide it so his arm wraps around my middle. "I just really enjoy this moment, soaking and relaxing with you." Turning to him I add, "I should have said it's a close second."

Owen takes the wine glass from its perch next to the tub. "I look forward to this all week, too."

We're both in our own thoughts, so it's a couple of peaceful minutes before I say, "Sky let it slip that Garth and Sienna are paying eight hundred dollars a month for their place, and when I looked up comps, units like theirs usually go for around six hundred."

"I don't know what the going rate is down there, but their place needs a lot of work. Did you feel how drafty it was by their windows the other night? I can't imagine what it's like when the temperature dips below zero." After taking another sip he puts his wine glass down and shifts his body to sit more upright. "You went on real estate sites to look up comps?"

I nod, feeling slightly uncomfortable. Owen has been pretty out in the open about his desire for me to move in, but we've never set a plan in place. Not out loud, anyway. But I definitely have a plan when it comes to us, and I'm certain he does too.

"All right," he starts in cautiously, "so does this mean you're making a decision about September?"

"I thought that was clear...I'm definitely putting in my resignation right after spring break so they have time to interview for a replacement."

"You mentioned it, but I didn't want to press you, or pressure you."

"Speak your mind with me, Owen. I'm becoming an open book, so let's not leave things unsaid, all right?"

He kisses the side of my neck before saying, "If we're saying what's in our hearts, then I want to make it clear that I'd love for you to move in here with me."

And it's hard, this communication thing, because my instinct is to hem and haw, to hedge so that I don't come off as a girl making assumptions. *Screw it*, I tell myself, *you're too old to be playing games.*

Straightening up, I turn to face him. "I want to live here with you."

And with a hopeful smile that melts my heart, he asks, "How soon can you move in?"

I love this man.

And he loves me.

# Chapter Thirty-Seven

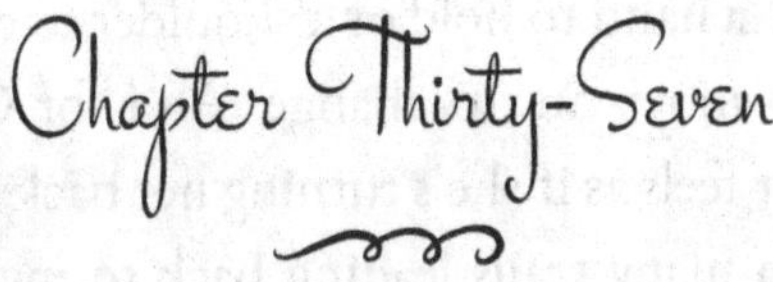



*SIX MONTHS LATER...*

## OWEN

It's not lost on me, the fact that we're standing in the same exact place we were last year at the beginning of September.

I'm not feeling exposed the way I was that night though, walking into this backyard with flowers in my shaking hands, praying I wasn't about to be sent off with my heart crushed.

Grace began the gradual process of moving in with me last spring, and to say we've learned a lot about each other in the past few months would be an understatement. I've learned she's a Scrabble master, she's fond of eating all foods straight from their containers, and that the woman has cold hands and cold feet in the morning—I'm talking shockingly frigid. But I'll take those cold limbs wrapping around me in bed any day of the week.

More than anything, being with Grace, day in and day out, has made me realize just how lonely I was before I met her.

I'm not saying it's been all sunshine and roses. Between the actual move, and dealing with everything that *moving on* signifies for Grace, the past few months have been hard. I'm honored that she's come to lean on me when she needs support, advice, a hand to hold or a shoulder to cry on.

It's hard to move on, to change. And for Grace I'm sure some part of her feels as if she's turning her back on her past.

She's left so many trails leading back to my house—make that *our* house—that if her daughter does come looking for her someday, I don't see how she could fail to find us. Let's just say that the staff at the post office, both here and at our local Pittsburgh branch, know Grace by face and by name.

Grace also contacted the agency that handled the adoption, updated her address on her university's alumni registry, and conned her sweet-natured school secretary into giving out her personal contact information to anyone who asks for it—a clear breach of the school's human resources policy.

The child she gave up will always live in her heart, just as the idea of our own child lives in mine.

I've bitten my tongue so many times. I didn't want to come off as selfish or insensitive, and most of all I didn't want her to run. But you can't live your life hiding what's in your heart.

"You can say it, you know."

"Say what?" I acted confused, although I know Grace must have caught the joy in my expression as I held Rose, Sienna and Garth's baby, at the party after she was baptized.

"You can ask me if I want children someday."

I shook my head. "It's not important, Grace. I'm just happy to have you."

"You're a terrible liar." I was relieved to see her cracking a smile when she added, "I guess that's a good quality."

My answer was at least half true. I *was* thrilled to have her back in my life.

"Grace, I do...I want *us* to have a child, but I know your feelings are complicated, and I've accepted that you might not ever be ready, or even want another child." We were both quiet for a moment before I cautiously added, "But any child would be blessed to have you as their mother. I know that for a fact."

She had tears in her eyes, but put her hand up to hold me off when I moved in to hug her.

"For a long time, whenever I let my mind go there, there was some voice inside of me saying, 'You don't deserve it.' Like, I gave up my child, so I'm not entitled to that kind of blessing or happiness anymore. But I've stopped beating myself up. Now, even if I don't feel it one hundred percent, I make a habit of looking at myself in the mirror and saying, *I love you.*" She stopped to laugh. "Don't worry, I say it in the quiet of my own mind...I don't want you thinking you shacked up with a cuckoo."

I wasn't smiling though, because I knew Grace didn't truly love herself for a long time, and the image of her looking in the mirror trying to convince herself that she's worthy broke my damn heart.

Grace came closer and took my hands in hers. "I'm almost there, Owen. Now when I look at myself, I don't turn away on reflex, and I've forgiven that twenty-year-old. She was scared and thought she was alone. Punishing myself has gotten me nowhere, I know that now. And I deserve good things, I truly believe that. I deserve a good man like you and I deserve a good life."

"I intend to give you the best of everything in this life."

"I know you do, and I want to give you every happiness, too."

*She makes everything better*, that's what I'm thinking when I catch sight of her.

My Grace is wearing a smile that's infectious tonight, looking on as Garth and Sienna host their guests in this home she made possible for them.

They've already put their stamp on the place. A swing set has been added to the backyard, in addition to a kiddie-sized basketball hoop that James could probably dunk on now. And the kids' room is painted pale green for the time being, but Garth has mentioned putting on a small addition so that the girls will eventually have their own room. Yep, girls plural—they just found out the sex of the baby.

We're surrounded by close friends tonight and the warmth of family. Skylar blushes every time someone admires the sparkly rock on her left hand, and we take turns nodding and taking it all very seriously when Olivia rattles off her list of junior bridesmaid's duties to anyone who'll listen.

Looking around, I take stock of our friends and acknowledge that we're all in a time of transition. Change is the one constant in this life we're given.

I'm feeling grateful and blessed already, but my heart nearly cracks wide open when I catch sight of Grace opening her arms to take Rose from a very busy Sienna. I try to school my expression as the woman I love cradles that sweet baby, but I can't help myself. It's my dream for our future come to life.

And then I'm asking her to say it again, because I'm not sure if I was lost in a fantasy just a moment ago when Grace caught my eye and smiled as she whispered, "I'm ready."

* * *

# A Note From Lily

Thank you for reading *Ghost on the Shore*. I hope you enjoyed reading Grace's story of love, loss, and second chances. Moms shouldn't pick favorites, but she is one of my all-time favorite characters.

What happened to the little girl she gave up so many years ago? The fourth and final book in the Blackbird series is up next: *All Your Life*. Meet Sarah Hamilton, although you may know her better as Birdie...

**Sarah Hamilton is living the dream.**
She earns perfect grades, has the right set of friends and wears the right clothes. She's a golden child, and the long-awaited answer to her parents' prayers.

I walk through that life—Sarah's life—every day, but it's like I'm watching from some perch on a tree outside the window. I'm always searching for something: some feeling, some connection, some person. I don't know who or what it is. All I know is that I don't belong.

I've known it all my life.

So when I finally discover what I've always known in my heart to be true, the words hit with the force of a freight train, leave me hollowed out and numb. But those same words?
**They also set me free.**

Also by Lily Foster

## THE LET ME SERIES

Let Me Be the One

Let Me Love You

Let Me Go

Let Me Heal Your Heart

Let Me Fall

When I Let You Go

## THE BLACKBIRD SERIES

When the Night is Over

Your Hand in Mine

Ghost on the Shore

All Your Life

www.ingramcontent.com/pod-product-compliance
Lightning Source LLC
Chambersburg PA
CBHW010509100726
47902CB00011B/2148